Run For Roses

James Rose

Books by James Rose

Chung Piece
Boo Hoff
Run For Roses

For my brother Trevor

We don't take a trip. A trip takes us.

~

John Steinbeck

RUN FOR ROSES

OCTOBER 30, 2018

Tomorrow, Meko and Foxworth go. I'll sure miss them here on the ranch. Especially Foxworth. We haven't been apart in...ever, I don't think. I think of him as a brother, even though we are not at all related. Together we arrived at the SPCA. Together we were adopted by Sunny to live on his ranch. The Milk River ranch we came from before was a nightmare. Life at the SPCA for an entire winter wasn't exactly peachy either, but beggars can't be choosers. I'm still getting used to our new names. Sunny said he wanted us to have handles that spoke of the "Dear Old Southland." When he told me that, I simply shrugged.

Today, Meko could see I was anxious. He said, "Lula Mae, writing a journal is cathartic. I suggest you try." He said he writes in his all the time. So, this here is my first journal. I'm glad he decided to help Sunny with har-vest. I'm happy he was here for Thanksgiving.

I'll have to trust Sunny. He said Foxworth needs adventure. What an op-portunity for him to join Meko on the road wherever it is they're going. I don't even think Sunny knows their destination. Maybe Meko doesn't ei-ther. Foxworth and I are similar in many ways. We're also quite different. From day one, it was clear he burns for seeing, doing, exploring. To live boldly. Whereas I'm happy to help out on the ranch. It's breathtaking out here. I'm okay living at 3/4 time. Besides, Sunny said he could always use a hand.

It was obvious Sunny enjoyed catching up with Meko. They hadn't seen each other since their road trip last spring through the Deep South. Two weeks ago, the whole family got together for Thanksgiving. I overheard

Sunny at the dinner table. He said he picked us up from the SPCA the week after he returned from New York. Meko laughed. He didn't think Sunny would actually do it. Sunny said, "You don't remember me telling you?" Meko said he didn't. He winked at me as he said it.

I made Foxworth promise to write me letters. I sure hope he does. Anyway, I feel better already. I think I'll stop writing now. Do I have to write one tomorrow? Do I sign my own journal? I guess there are no rules. Anyway, I should get to bed. Sunny said we have to bail hay all day tomorrow. He said, "Miss Lula Mae, tomorrow we ride at dawn."

OCTOBER 31

Dear Lula Mae,

I don't know where we will be on our road trip by the time this reaches you. But I will make sure that wherever we stop for a night, I will write you a letter. I wasn't sure exactly why we left, and I'm not sure if you know, but can you believe we're gone? We made it as far as Seattle today. It was a long day. I hope you aren't missing us too much. Seattle is only a day's drive away from Alberta, which may put things in perspective. I mean, we could be on an airplane nearing the other side of the world by now. But no, we are a day's drive away.

Anyway, enough about all that. I'll be back home soon. Might be a few months, who knows. Tonight is Halloween. Meko went out with friends. He didn't say when they'd be back. They're trusting that I don't do any damage while they are out trick or treating or whatever it is they do.

I may as well start describing what happened today. And I have some good news to share, but I'll get to that in a moment. First, let me just say the drive across the state of Washington, it's long and straight. Of course, we could've taken the smaller roads off the interstate to head west, but Meko made the right call to stay on the interstate and haul ass. We drove for at least ten hours today. I am exhausted. After we left Alberta, we drove down and crossed near Yahk in BC.

Meko was telling stories of the time he worked for a summer in the town of Yahk. That is if you can call Yahk a town. It's tiny. He said it was one of the most physically challenging jobs he's ever had. All day, every day, he was in the mountains walking in dead straight lines, every few metres digging a hole beneath the topsoil and bagging the dirt. By the end of the day, he said his pack was never less than one hundred pounds. And the line he had to walk, it had to be straight. It didn't matter if there was a cliff in the way, a steep slope covered in a tangle of alder, or a raging river to cross. The line had to be maintained. The company he was working for was on the hunt for a zinc mine. Something like that anyway.

He said it was also one of the most enjoyable summers he's ever had. He told one story of how one of his coworkers snuck into an empty room in the roadside motel they lived in for the summer. Well, one night, a guy walked up to the motel in the wee hours, drunkern hell, and he thought his girlfriend, the manager, was still living in the motel. This guy wasn't aware that she was no longer at the motel because, only days earlier, she fled with their kids. She knew he was on the lookout for her. There was a restraining order he had to abide by. So, he barges into the motel room Meko's co-worker is sleeping in. It's the middle of the night, and what does the guy see? Another guy in his old bed. Meko was laughing so hard he couldn't finish the rest of the story. All he said was that no one got hurt and Ben got to keep his motel room.

It didn't take long to cross into the US. The border patrol officer didn't even bother to see if my food was sealed. He just waved us through and voilà, Montana. Meko rolled down the window, turned the music up and said we would be in San Francisco in no time. We didn't even stop; we just kept driving all the way from the border down to Spokane. In Spokane, we went for a walk through the downtown area, and I took my time to stretch my legs, go for a pee.

Meko was hungry and so was I. It was maybe around noon when we arrived. We didn't stay long after we ate. We proceeded to saddle up and head west toward the Pacific, through Washington's hot, arid interior. The best part about it, without question, is the drive alongside the mighty Columbia. It's quite something how much the river widens down here. And the topography, so different from the Columbia River wetlands near the river's headwaters. Meko and I drove through that part of BC before crossing the border.

I am excited about tomorrow, or the next day, when our next stop after Seattle is Astoria, Oregon. That's where the Columbia empties into the Pacific Ocean. Imagine that, all the way from Columbia Lake in southeast BC, the river travels, widens, and then eventually flows into the Pacific. If the river wasn't dammed, we might've been lucky to see the salmon run on our road trip today. Before the dams were built, salmon would spawn from the ocean to Columbia Lake each fall. That's thousands of kilometres of against the current swimming.

Before we went over the Snoqualmie Pass to arrive in Seattle, we stopped in Ellensburg. This was an essential stop for Meko. He said he had family history in the town and that it would be his first time ever visiting. When we arrived, we were in luck: the rodeo was on! This, the very rodeo that one of Meko's great grandpa's used to compete after the second world war. I think I can speak for us both in saying how surprised we were at how country Ellensburg is. They are proud of their country roots. Country music, rodeos, cowboy boots, so very different from liberal urban Seattle just over the hill.

Before going to the rodeo, we visited the Ellensburg high school. Meko said that it was from that same school his great grandpa graduated from all those years ago. He never went to college and moved up to northern Alberta to be a trapper after high school. I think this is where Meko gets his thirst to roam and explore and see new. His great-grandpa was a cowboy, logger and farmer across western Canada and the USA. And he read all kinds of books: fiction, science, social science, and on and on.

The rodeo was genuine. Small, traditional, family oriented. What we observed: young families, humble competitions like heaviest pig, horse cutting, a variety of livestock and lots of candy. It was a hot day. It wasn't wild and crazy; it was reserved. The only music was fiddles and things played by men and women in overalls with hair braids. I loved it. I was hoping we would stay for the night. But Meko wanted to get on the road and go as far as Seattle. It would save us money and his friend we would be staying with had plans for Halloween. I wasn't optimistic the evening agenda would include me. Sure enough, it didn't. The silver lining is that I have time to write you this letter while they are out.

I forgot to mention, there was a period of our drive between Spokane and Ellensburg where it looked like we were doomed. Meko didn't think we needed to fill the tank with gas when we got to Spokane. I wasn't checking the gauge, but I trusted his judgement. Meko wanted to get out of rough and tumble Spokane before stopping for gas. I do not know how the car didn't die on us. It was on E and the dash said there were zero litres left in the tank despite the vehicle still running. Meko checked Maps on his phone to find the nearest gas station. It was fifty kilometres away when we noticed the gas gauge had forty odd kilometres remaining. To make matters worse, it was a hilly part of the interstate. On the downs, he was in neutral. He sat on a low gear on the ups, kept the RPM's at two and my goodness, did we sweat it out. Running out of gas would've thrown a major kink into the trip's overall mojo. The time it would take to figure out how to get more gas on the side of the interstate, the fatigue we were already feeling from a full day of driving, it was all unpleasant. But...we made it. That car, while I'm happy that it came through in the end, clearly the gauge isn't accurate. But enough about gas and the car. It's a gem. It's our ticket to San Francisco. I will not speak ill of the car again.

Okay, time for the good news. Somewhere between Spokane and Sprague, Meko promised me that this road trip would be the perfect opportunity for him to tell the story of how he and his cousin (your Sunny), who he thinks of as his brother, made it from New Orleans to Louisville, Kentucky. I never asked for the story. He offered to tell it. I don't think he's told anyone, nor has Sunny. I also don't think he appreciates that I will be writing you these letters. But it is my belief that it is my responsibility to record this story. I will do my best to remember all that he said. And I will do my best to give him the benefit of the doubt when he tells the story. You never know with him. He said, "Foxworth, I think it's time I try and piece together how and why that road trip happened. You're my audience, whether you like it or not." And then he started. He put the Spotify playlist on that he and Sunny listened to on their road trip to get him in the mood. He started from the beginning.

So, here's my goal Lula Mae. In the letters I write to you each time we stop for a night, you will read about the road trip Meko and I are on. You will also read about the far more exciting road trip that Meko and Sunny took last Spring from Louisiana to Kentucky. I am hoping that you and I will finally understand by the time we get to San Francisco what the hell happened on that trip. The way that I want to write Meko's story down will be the same way he tells it to me. While you read my letters, don't forget that it's Meko telling the story. He's telling it from his perspective. A reliable account? Who knows. Entertaining and factual can be mutually exclusive.

Without further ado, I will now try my best to write down what Meko told me today between Sprague and Seattle. Of course, while we were at the rodeo, he didn't keep telling the story. He said it was meant for my ears only and only for our time spent in the car. He continued orating from Ellensburg over the Snoqualmie Pass to Seattle. Another time I'll tell you more about that part of the drive. Oh and one more thing. Remember how much we enjoyed listening to the audiobook of John Steinbeck's *Tortilla Flat*? Remember how before each chapter, there were a couple sentences that read like: How Danny, home from the wars, found himself an heir, and how he swore to protect the helpless. How Jesus Maria Corcoran, a good man, became an unwilling vehicle of evil. I want to try framing Meko's story told orally to me in the same fashion.

Anyway, here goes...

Best,
Foxworth

* * *

How the cousins who thought of themselves as brothers arrived in New Orleans, a city they fell in love with. And how they were sprung to action after a fateful phone call concerning the poor health of a dear friend.

This is the story of how I, Meko Torres, along with my dear cousin Sunny, who I think of as a brother, got from New Orleans to Louisville, Kentucky in the months of April and May, in the year 2018. The purpose of the trip was mainly to save someone's life. We didn't know if we could pull it off. And since no one has heard this story, I'll keep the ending, whether we succeeded or not, for the end.

Since there was a tremendous uncertainty over whether we would accomplish our goal, Sunny and I decided that we would dedicate the style of the road trip to the person whose life we were hoping to save. His name, Von Rotz. What that meant was for us to experience the land between those two cities. And by experience, I mean to see and to taste and to drink it all in.

We wanted to get the soil of each place between our fingernails. We wanted to meet people. We wanted to get drunk, see the countryside, listen to the local music, eat the local food. We wanted to live the road trip like it would be our last. That was the way Von Rotz had taught us to live our lives. Time and again through our childhood, Von Rotz was the one to not just tell us how. He showed us. Those stories, maybe I will try and include in this story. I'm not sure. Maybe for another road trip.

Sunny and I met in New Orleans. Our original intention was to only go for the New Orleans Jazz and Heritage Festival. That was it. We had no idea what kind of shit was about to come our way. And I'll get to that. But let me start from the beginning.

I arrived from New Orleans from San Diego Friday evening. Sunny and I had spent the last few days in San Diego, where we met after our own solo trips in California. While I was at a music festival in the desert east of Los Angeles, Sunny had flown to San Francisco and driven his way down the Pacific Coast Highway to arrive in San Diego, where he and I met. For a few days, we enjoyed that city together. We stayed at a hostel in Ocean Beach. It was clean and cheap. I liked it and I think Sunny did too.

Both our little vacations were going to end with us attending Jazz Fest. Months prior, we bought our weekend tickets. We had already purchased our plane tickets to get from San Diego over to Louisiana and from Louisiana, home. Me to Taos, Sunny to Okotoks. We both always look for the cheapest, most convenient airfare. That was why he arrived to New Orleans earlier than me on a different flight. When I finally arrived in the Big Easy, Sunny already had spent the day there.

I met him at the hostel we had booked on the corner of the French Quarter. It was expensive. The owners jack the prices up for their meagre quality lodgings to take advantage of the surging demand during Jazz Fest. I think we were paying almost two hundred each night for rickety beds in a big dorm room. Our room was crowded. But it was also lots of fun.

The first thing Sunny and I did was go for food in New Orleans. Food in New Orleans. It's a place where what you eat isn't just calories. There's much more to it. There are decades worth of gumbo pot cultural influence in every bite. In every dish. And there are lots of different dishes. What's also true is that in New Orleans, during Jazz Fest, you will be waiting in line to sit down at any of the French Quarter restaurants.

Though I suppose what the busyness did do was push us into new culinary directions. We didn't fall for the low hanging fruit of what's known and advertised as premier examples of New Orleans cuisine. If we wanted to be expedient with our dining, we needed to find the little hole in the wall, out of the way places. The places that haven't had Anthony Bourdain type characters blow the lid off on why this particular joint run by grandma in her eighties is so freaking great. The kind of place with plastic chairs, fluorescent lighting, disposable plates and cutlery. The sort of place where the only way they have a chance of making a go is to serve cuisine of the highest order. These places don't have a budget for marketing gimmicks. All they have is a devotion to gratefully serving their customers their best version of a dish. Their best version of gumbo, red beans and rice, jambalaya or étouffée. These places are not easy to find. There aren't many of them. And it's hard to know if you've found one in the first place. Ours are not the most discerning of palates.

In any event, if that mythic beast of an eating establishment ever did cross our tracks, there was one restaurant we did find that may have lived up to the idyllic description I just provided. But we didn't get to that place until Saturday night. If I remember correctly, on Friday night, we had our dinner at the Jazz Fest grounds. We each had a couple Po-boys. We drank light beer. Come to think of it, maybe that was The Meal.

We were there more for the music, anyway. At least I was. The food was the icing on a big cake. A vast, rich, beautiful cake. Sunny and I, we have different tastes in music. There is some common ground, but for the most part, we diverge. Whereas I was more interested in John Boutté type figures, Sunny wanted, well, he wasn't sure what he wanted. Maybe that's the more accurate way to differentiate our tastes in music. Mine, it's deliberate. His, I think, is passive. To Sunny, music is for the background. It was the scene that demanded more of his attention. And there sure was a scene. Sunny had lots of reasons for his way of thinking. The personalities, the clothes, the diversity of it all. It was a scene to behold. Not just at Jazz Fest, but throughout the city. I think it's fair to say that New Orleans isn't the southernmost North American city but the northernmost South American city.

This wasn't the first time for me in New Orleans. The previous year I went with Jobe, the same guy we're staying with here in Seattle. That trip was mind blowing good. I believe visiting New Orleans for the first time is truly a unique experience. And I was lucky to do it during Jazz Fest. The best act I saw was Tom Petty. Not long after that performance, Petty died from an opiate overdose. I was pretty down when I heard that news. I never would've guessed he had those kinds of issues based on the performance he gave. It seemed like every song he and the Heartbreakers played was a hit. His catalogue is enormous! Standing next to us was a couple in their forties from Queens, New York. We got along really well. I can't remember their names, but the boyfriend had seen Petty something like forty times through the years. He was wearing a Yankees hat and he kind of looked like Derek Jeter. His girlfriend talked and talked and talked. I didn't mind it.

The group of people in front of us were our age. They were getting hammered and we ordered many drinks together during the show. One of the guys was wearing a Montana hat and they were all wearing clothes with brands like Patagonia and North Face. I just assumed that's where they were all from, Montana. Nope, all of them were from the New Orleans area. After Petty, I asked the guy who'd seen him forty-one times now how the show ranked. To my surprise, he said he'd seen better. To me, it was one of the best shows I'd ever seen. Can't imagine what Jeter had seen in the past.

I'll just tell one more story from that trip before I continue Run For Roses. That's my own little name for the trip Sunny and I did. It's the story of partying with a Jazz Fest performer who I won't name at the Harrah's Casino later that night. Before we went to the Petty show, we went to this one hit wonder's performance. Her hit, it's a good one. She's a punk rocker. At the end of her set, she announced to the crowd that she was going to Harrah's later that night. My buddy and I, we looked at each other and shrugged. Maybe that's where we would end up too. Between Petty and Harrah's, where we eventually did go, lots happened that I can't recall all that well. We ate too much food, we drank one too many grenades and then there we were in Harrah's, looking for Princess Punk. I found her. I snuck behind the ropes of a VIP area and there she was with her entourage.

At the blackjack table, Princess Punk was showing her true colours. She was acting like a total diva. I was totally turned off. Jobe however, was loving it. He and the Princess got along great. When a Louis Armstrong song came on, they fox trotted! And then all of us sudden, the Princess had to go. Her manager approached her and whispered in her ear that she had another engagement across town at the Maple Leaf. Jobe and I hoped we could join, but they left without us. From Harrah's, we went back to the Quarter and I think we spent the rest of that night at the Apple Bar on Frenchman Street listening to a jam band from New Jersey. Waiting On Mongo, the band's name. Outstanding music and these guys were just getting going on their careers. No big record deals or management or publicity.

Anyway, I should mention that southern Louisiana at the end of April is a fine place to be when it's not raining. That first Friday evening for Sunny and I, it was dry and cloudless. The afternoon sun's intensity had softened, the humidity was low. It was comfortable. Sunny and I found the row of food vendors and went straight to the one with the shortest line. Music from the many festival stages came in varying directions. The closest was a blues-centric stage. Whichever band was playing was deep into a swampy slide guitar set. The Creole singer was howlin' for lost love. Above the cashier, Sunny noticed a sign that read: Ain't Nothin' a Po-boy Can't Fix. We ordered two crawfish Po-boys each.

Sting was the main draw that night. He came on stage looking like he was thirty-five when in fact, he's pushing seventy. Any questions the crowd may have had about his singing abilities, if he could still hit the high notes (which was every note), immediately, they were put to rest. Sunny and I were completely transfixed. After God knows how many hits he played, then came *I'm an Englishman in New York*. My personal favourite. Sting nailed it. I think we both thought if that was the last show we'd ever see, that'd be fine.

After Sting, we went back to the Quarter. The next place that I want to tell you about is very special to Sunny and me. Of course, I had gone the previous year with Jobe and knew that Sunny would love it. On Decatur Street and the corner of Jackson Square in New Orleans, along the banks of the Mississippi River, I took Sunny to the Café du Monde. The original French market, since 1862.

Café du Monde is open twenty-four hours a day, every single day save for Christmas Day and when the occasional hurricane passes. It is old and steeped in tradition. It's been written about, it's been sung about. The menu has chicory coffee, beignets, a few cold drinks, and...that's it. A wonderful example of less is more. The prices are surprisingly low, even to an experienced tourist used to being bilked. There's a small counter to place orders and the menu is posted on the wall. The many employees wear tidy uniform: white button-up dress shirt, white apron, black bow-tie, branded paper hat, and of course, a smile. They are all exceedingly polite. You walk underneath the green and white striped awning and you think, I'll never get served. Too many people, utter chaos. But no, you are served almost immediately. You either go to the counter, or you find yourself a little circular table, plop yourself down, and wait. You people watch. From all over the country and world. Eating their powdered sugar coated beignets (a cross between a fritter and a doughnut). Drinking black chicory coffee or better yet, a café au lait. You may start sweating in the heat. You may start conversing with total strangers. You may sit silent and watch as a boat makes its way down the old river. There's an overweight fella across the street. He's set up on a stool with his giant tuba. His friend will arrive shortly with a clarinet and they'll play old songs, new songs. A Professor Longhair tune, and then a Hoagy Carmichael. They take their time.

The next day, we explored east New Orleans. We started along St. Charles Avenue on our old jalopy rental bikes, haulin' ass, hair in the wind. The shades were on and we weaved in and out of traffic. We passed through district after district moving east. Pretty women in canary yellow dresses, bright red walking shoes, large sunglasses and felt brimmed hats walked their dogs. In the middle of St. Charles, a streetcar clattered by. The sun was getting warmer with each passing hour. By lunchtime, we had reached Audubon Park and it was there we decided to take a break. Sunny found a café in the shade. We parked our bikes and took a load off.

We talked about what else we wanted to see that day. I'd heard of a place called Tipitina's, a legendary music venue. Sunny was game and off we went on our search. It took a while to find it, but eventually we did. On the corner of Napoleon and Tchoupitoulas is Tipitina's. I knew of the eponymous song, a New Orleans classic, I heard on a Dr. John record. I had to see this place. Not much to look at with its pale yellow clapboard exterior, but the sounds coming from within! There was a long line out front to get in. You didn't need to be inside to hear it. Sunny and I saved money and time and enjoyed it from the outside. Most people around us had Jazz Fest wristbands on and were well on their way to another wild day and night. To my surprise, Sunny led the charge. He went to a nearby food truck and ordered highballs.

Eventually, we arrived back at the festival. For a brief period, we split. I went to the Louis Prima tribute. Sunny met up with me there later. When he got there, I was leading a woman onto the dance floor. It was a woman of Louis' generation. She was elderly and Sunny watched as I delicately fox trotted with this game old Italian bird.

Someone else may have looked at that and thought, what a nice grandson. Sunny was maybe the only one to know that she wasn't my grandmother. At what I was doing, I don't think he was surprised. Sunny stood on the edge of the dance floor. A big smile overtook his face. What he saw was me dancing with keen focus, eyes closed. After the song, everyone clapped and hollered at the music and the unique pair of dancers. I hugged grandma, she gave me a kiss on the cheek. "Grazie cara," she said with a wink.

Aretha Franklin's show, Saturday's headliner, was canceled. There was confusion as to why at first, but then it became known among us festival goers that it had something to do with her health. We found out on our way to get a drink after a soul-reviving experience at the gospel tent. Had we not just been saved by Him, we may have felt more remorse over not seeing the soul legend perform. At the gospel tent, I never ended up on stage, but by the end of the Zulu Gospel Ensemble's show, my hands were up, my eyes were closed, and I was professing my love for the Lord Almighty. Sunny was past the point of no return now with his liquor intake and was at the back of the tent, running from one side to the other while the singers sang.

Black and white and young and old were infected with the singer's ability to command the crowd. The vibe was pure salvation. He was a master conductor at the front of the Train of God. Lord have mercy! Come to the Promised Land! Can I get a witness? Sunny was running toward the Promised Land. I was humming and singing back up vocal. For forty-five minutes, we went wild. Everyone under that giant tent went wild. Sting was a sleeper compared to this.

When it was over, there was a prayer. It went quiet. Bonnie Raitt's guitar could be heard from another stage, but the crowd had their heads low and listened to the Zulu frontman give one last sermon. When he was finished, people were hugging, tears were streaming down faces. Sunny and I, our eyes glistened. We hugged each other and then with complete strangers. The dream came true! Without Aretha to go to, we decided on Jack Johnson. When we got to his stage, beach balls were floating around the crowd and Jack, singing about banana pancakes, sounded just like he did on his records.

After Jack, we walked almost four miles from the festival to the Roosevelt Hotel. To walk would give us a chance to see another part of the city, talk, and maybe sober up a little. Sunny and I didn't make it far after exiting before finding ourselves inside, along with many others, the home of a complete stranger. There was a massive house party taking place and everyone was welcome. A jam band was wailing away in the front driveway and people were dancing, drinking and eating their faces off.

Outside the house, there was a moveable feast. A couple guys had rolled a trailer out front, which had two big barbecues on it made from recycled propane tanks. A menu board was attached to one of the four beams holding the makeshift roof over the chef's head. "Ghetto BBQ," the name of the business.

The smells coming off the grill, the alcohol induced hunger, Sunny and I didn't stand a chance holding our appetites. Sunny ordered blackened jerk chicken straight off the grill. I ordered a double hamburger with bacon. There were a few stools set up on the sidewalk, and we sat and ate and said little. After a few bites, we looked at each other, chewing, eyebrows raised, eyes slightly bloodshot. Sunny was about to say something, but I went for another bite. No need to talk. Sunny ordered a burger after he was finished. I ordered another sausage. "I'm gonna roll all the way to the Roosevelt," I said. "But so be it."

When we were done, back into the house party we went. Festival goers were still streaming out from the nearby exits. Sunny pointed out that he liked Jazz Fest because it didn't go past seven at night. That meant there was plenty of time after to hit the town. In fact, some of the best shows happened afterward in New Orleans clubs and theatres. Later that night, for example, Trombone Shorty had a sold out show at Preservation Hall. Across town at the Maple Leaf Bar, Jon Boutté also performed to a sold out crowd. On more than one occasion, I overheard people say Boutté was New Orleans' finest singing son.

It was dark when we got to the Roosevelt. It was a long walk made longer by our inability to maintain a straight line. I thought that after a Sazerac or two, we'd be done for the evening. The previous night, I only managed three hours of sleep before my morning run. I was exhausted. But I didn't share these thoughts with Sunny. The long walk was an excellent chance for us to speak our minds in a drunken stupor. And while we could've just as quickly gone down the windy road of the serious things in life, we chose not to.

We talked about music. I was keen to share my thoughts on why this festival of almost fifty years was what every festival should aspire to. Sunny agreed but also lamented the absence of EDM. He liked that stuff and figured he'd probably be having a better time at Coachella or Electric Daisy Carnival. Having just been to Coachella, I couldn't understand it. But then Sunny couldn't understand the fuss about seeing a tribute to Louis Prima sung by his daughter. An argument was about to rear its ugly head, but then somehow, cooler heads prevailed and we moved on to a different subject. Food. We both could agree that as far as cities went, New Orleans may take the cake. We wagered a bet on how many pounds we would gain in our three days in the city. I thought five pounds. Sunny thought seven.

At the Roosevelt, I asked the concierge where to find the finest Sazerac in all the land. He pointed us toward the *Sazerac Bar* across the hall. The bartenders, the interior decor, the clientele, everything about it oozed class.

The John Legend show had just finished across the street at the Orpheum Theater. The Sazerac Bar at the Hotel Roosevelt hosted the unofficial afterparty. Sunny got in line at the bar, I ducked out to the restroom. When I came back, I found Sunny in an increasingly intimate conversation with a lovely woman twice his age. Sunny, with his Sundance Kid good looks. That's how I gave him his nickname. His real name, I won't reveal. I went to the bar to give Sunny space. I ordered a Sazerac and asked the bartender to give me a little history lesson.

"It's America's first cocktail," she said. "Created right here in New Orleans. First made in 1838 in the French Quarter by a man named Antoine Peychaud. He named the drink after his favourite French brandy – Sazerac-de-Forge et Fils."

"Come again?" I asked.

"Sazerac-de-Forge et Fils. It's French."

"Yeah, I get that. Anyway, continue..."

"Later, after the Civil War, a bartender named Leon Lamothe added absinthe and replaced cognac with American Rye whiskey. But in 1912, absinthe was banned, so Peychaud replaced it with his special bitters. When absinthe was made legal again, they added it back and now what we have is the following...enjoy."

Now, I could keep telling you, scene-by-scene, what happened in New Orleans that weekend. All that happened leading up to the fateful phone call. But I don't want to bore you. The critical thing to know is that Sunny and I were having us a grand ol' time. Sunny and I later agreed that it was right about the point we hit a New Orleanian climax that he got the call. It was a phone call that changed our lives. We were on Frenchman Street. It was Sunday night and this was supposed to be our last night in the city.

The next day, we both had flights booked out of Louis Armstrong International. Sunny was on his way home to Alberta and I was returning to Taos.

The Jimmy Buffett headliner show that night was good, not great. Speaking of Buffett, I have to share a few thoughts on him before I get to the call that changed our lives. I understand the draw of Buffett. I'm a fan. I first heard of him from a hero of mine, my mother's first cousin... so he would be a first cousin, once removed? Anyway, Darren was the one to turn me onto a bunch of great music when I was a kid. Before my teenage years. I distinctly remember the day, when we were at our family cottage for Thanksgiving many years ago, when he asked Sunny and me whether we'd heard of the Allman Brothers. I told him no. He couldn't believe it and then played us *Ramblin' Man, Blue Sky, Melissa*. I was hooked. Whenever Darren and his family came out to the country to visit from the coast, he brought his songbook and an acoustic guitar. It was thrilling because he was so good to listen to sing and play.

On one of those Thanksgivings, Darren played Margaritaville. He had a newborn at the time, who just graduated high school last year, and he changed the lyrics when we were all singing along. Buffett's lyrics go like this: "Some people claim that there is a woman to blame, but I know, it's my own damn fault." Darren changed it to, "Some people claim that there is a baby to blame..." As we sang, the baby was crawling across the carpet, smiling, giggling. It was magic.

Anyway, for moments like those, that's why I think the world needs more guys like Jimmy Buffett. Of course, he doesn't need to keep touring, at least not for the money. But still, he does. His story, the whole Margaritaville thing, I get it. The ironic thing about my relationship with Jimmy Buffett is that I like his records more than his live show. And he's a live act. Not all of his records, only a few he put out in the 70s. For me, it starts with *White Sport Coat and a Pink Crustacean*. And then *Living and Dying in 3/4 Time*. I think his best was his next record, *A1A*.

But there's nothing new going on at a Jimmy Buffett show. It's tried and true. He only will play the same few songs. Sometimes, he'll let someone onstage do their own thing for a brief interlude. In our case, we were treated to the strange but talented Mac McNally. But still, standing in the crowd that night in New Orleans, I couldn't help but feel like I was at a museum exhibit for baby boomer escapism. I like the new new thing. I would much prefer a musician with a stable of hits to stretch out, try new and be vulnerable. I know, even after what I just told you about Tom Petty. But Petty and Buffett, that's a different argument.

Petty is one of those artists; his songs, the sound quality, enough for me to forgive the fact that everything we heard was decades old. The same goes, I suppose, for Sting. But then Sting's enduring appeal to me has more to do with him doing mind-blowing Tiny Desk Concerts on NPR with people like Shaggy.

Anyway, after the Buffett show, Sunny and I returned to the French Quarter. We ate big bowls of gumbo and went to the Carousel Bar at the Hotel Monteleone. We didn't think twice about spending over twenty bucks for a single cocktail at that bar. This was our last night in New Orleans and we were happy to splurge.

The phone call came later on. We were back on Frenchman Street. Frenchman, much better than Bourbon. Frenchman felt more local. Sunny and I were in the midst of a crowd outside. It was around one in the morning. There was a makeshift band of jazz guys on the street commanding everyone's attention. This type of show is the true essence of Jazz Fest. Forget the big budget headliners. Go to Jazz Fest for the street performers. This is their big showcase as much as anyone else's with all the people in town.

It was Sunny's mom. She called and told him that Von Rotz was sick. Sunny's sunburnt face went white when he heard the news. I watched it happen. He nodded his head, trying to listen to his mom while the band was playing and the crowd was cheering. Sunny took off down an alley. I followed to see what the hell was going on. At first, I lost him. But then I heard him calling out to me. I turned back and then he came out from an alley and told what was up.

"He's sick."

"Who is?"

"Von Rotz."

"Sick?"

"Yes, sick. It's bad."

"How bad?"

"Bad."

To my frustration, it took a while for me to pry the story out of Sunny. He was in shock. He eventually just let it all out. Von Rotz had cancer. He didn't have much time left. After telling me, we were made silent by our thoughts. Didn't speak for a long time.

I need to fill you in on Von Rotz and why he meant the world to us. He taught us many things. He took us on his old sailboat up and down the west coast. Showed us how to golf, hosted countless dinners and parties. He wasn't blood related but was a long time friend of the family. He was the kind of person people loved or hated. There was no in between. If he liked you, you knew it. It worked the other way too. He had chutzpah. He was in his late sixties. It was too soon for a guy like him to go down. Wasn't he playing tennis every day? He had one grown daughter in her fifty's. He smoked like a chimney.

The story goes, he dropped out of university after knocking up his girl-friend sophomore year. He was on an athletic scholarship at the University of Oregon. He was a runner and Bill Bowerman was his coach. Von Rotz said he used to hang with the Nike guys all the time back when it was Blue Ribbon. He knew Pre. After the pregnancy, he dropped out and went to work. He was fed up with the USA and went to Canada. He first went to Vancouver Island and then got a logging job on the mainland. At the age of twenty-two, he separated from the girl that gave him his one and only daughter, Shannon. Shannon and Von Rotz have had a strained relationship. It's not territory that Sunny and I ever really wished to wade into. That was his business, not ours.

Anyway, Von Rotz eventually wound up working as an investor for a non-profit organization with a sizeable endowment. I have no idea how he got into that line of work, but he was always travelling around doing his own funky kind of research on what was a smart investment. I have no idea whether he ever made any money or not. His work reputation was stellar. By the time I got to know him, he was in his forties and living on a sailboat. He would travel up and down the coast chasing the weather. In the summer months, he was in Canadian waters. In the winter months, he would travel south, sometimes as far as the Caribbean.

His sailboat, *Alysheba*, was a sixty footer. It was built in the 1980s and he loved that damn boat. The story of how he came to own the boat is classic Von Rotz. The boat was a result of a trip to Louisville, Kentucky. To Churchill Downs for the Kentucky Derby. It was 1987, and he said he knew next to nothing about horse racing. But she did. They had met in an airport, in one of those private lounge areas for people who pay. I think he said it was in Los Angeles. She was stunning. Her name was Chantal. She was on her way to the Derby and invited Von Rotz to join. She said there was serious money to be made this year on one particular horse, provided you knew a certain bet. Von Rotz was intrigued. She explained the situation that involved a horse called Alysheba. So, he changed his flight, changed his whole plan, and went along for the ride. Two birds one stone, Chantal and an investment opportunity. See, here was a guy who could let himself be spontaneous. That was a big lesson he never really talked about to Sunny and me. It was something we came to appreciate through observation.

RUN FOR ROSES · 33

The bet Chantal dreamt up, the one that she and Von Rotz placed, he never told how it worked. All he said was that it worked. With the money that he staked her, they won big. Alysheba won the Derby that year. Von Rotz didn't say how much he won, but he said it was with that money he bought his boat. Chantal was furious that he didn't name it after her and that was why their romance never flourished.

So there Sunny and I were, in New Orleans, at the end of April. Von Rotz was on his deathbed. This was all such news to us. We hadn't heard from him for quite some time. It was a mystery as to why he fell off the radar. Sunny and I were obviously no longer in any mood to continue our partying. We began to walk back to the hostel. As we walked, Sunny told me the rest of what his mother said.

Von Rotz sold *Alysheba* and had flown against his doctor's orders to a private British clinic to pay for experimental treatment. The treatment didn't work and Von Rotz was now in and out of a Vancouver hospital barely hanging on. How he got Canadian healthcare, I do not know. There are lots of things about the guy that I never will know. To Sunny and I, the loss of *Alysheba* had more to do with Von Rotz's declining health. That thing was a part of him. It was just like how you hear those stories of the husband passing only a year after a wife of 60 years passing, despite seemingly good health. Yes, Von Rotz had late-stage cancer, but we believed that he'd be in much better shape had he not sold his boat. To us, the boat was key to him having any shot of beating the Big C.

At around four or five in the morning, there we were on the back steps of our shotgun shack French Quarter hostel. As we watched the black night slowly brighten with the coming of dawn, I blurted an off the cuff remark about going to the Derby to see if we could win back the boat. Right as I said it, Sunny whirled around. We smiled at each other. Without question, that was what we had to do. I looked up when the next Derby was. It was only one week away. Were tickets still available? Sunny checked. Sure enough, there were a few still remaining for the infield. We didn't even know what that meant, the infield. Sunny bought two tickets to the Derby on his phone. Less than five minutes after I mentioned the idea of going to the Derby. That was how quick it all came together.

Of course, we didn't have to actually be in Churchill Downs to place a bet, but that was the way we were going to do it. There was no other acceptable way. Our mission would be a failure if we didn't place a bet in Churchill Downs. Would it be a failure if we failed to win enough to buy back the boat? Sunny and I never discussed that. The morning sun shone bright. It was Monday on the last day of April and we had until Saturday to get to Louisville.

* * *

That was how Meko left off when we arrived in Seattle. As you can imagine, all I want to do is get on the road and hear how the rest of this tale ends. But here I am, in Jobe's Capitol Hill apartment, with a roommate not all that happy I'm here. Tomorrow Meko said he was going to take me for a walk in a nearby park. Whether or not we will get on the road down to Astoria, I'm not sure. And like I said, I'm not even sure why we are on this trip in the first place down to San Francisco!

NOVEMBER 3

Dear Lula Mae,

I write this letter to you from Pacific City, Oregon. Meko and I arrived to this little beach town in the early evening. We had an incredible drive down from Seattle. I trust you got my first letter? In that letter, I think I said the plan was for us to stay in Astoria. We ended up visiting there but not lingering. A friend of Meko had told us that we needed to spend a night in Pacific City instead. It's only about an hour's drive south of Astoria. It's quiet and far less expensive.

Astoria, of course, had what you expect it would, the clapboard coastal look, but it's rougher than what I imagined. It's true, Oregon is grittier than Washington. I like that about this state. Maybe it's because we arrived there in the off-season that it came across a little less fake nice. You know what I mean about fake nice. It's the way city planners, government tourism organizations spruce up a place for the visitors. The grit is still there, but it gets swept under the rug. In Astoria and even Pacific City, the grit is in plain sight. I've been told there's a drugs problem in Oregon. You can see it on the streets, even in seaside places like Astoria. But with a place like Astoria, what you also get is a feeling of fantastic history. Here's the community nearest to the Columbia's mouth. I like the weather at this time of year in the Pacific Northwest. Although, to be fair, we've somehow avoided the rains. It's been overcast and it gets dark early. It's moody.

We left Seattle first thing in the morning today. Meko was good to show me around the city. We went to Pike Place Market, went to the Space Needle, went all over the place. At Pike Place, Meko had one of those guys selling giant fish throw him one. He didn't catch it and the fish exploded on the pavement because the guy, wearing these huge rubber gloves, threw it a clear twenty yards across the street! Meko prepaid for the fish and we took the shovelled remains in a bucket down to the docks. The birds had a nice feed.

I like Seattle. In Capitol Hill, where we stayed with Meko's friends, there are expensive coffee shops next to old record shops. In those record shops, you hear all kinds of music. The one we spent a few hours in was playing Aretha Franklin loud. It was in an old warehouse type building and the sound system was surprisingly good. Aretha played loud on vinyl in a Capitol Hill record store is an experience worth writing about. After, we went to the Museum of Pop Culture. That may be the coolest museum I'll ever go to. They have exhibits devoted entirely to the grunge music scene that the PNW is famous for. There's an exhibit devoted entirely to Jimi. And there are booths to play and record your own music. It's a cool place with funky architecture. We spent an entire afternoon at the museum. Never before have I done that. Paul Allen gave a bunch of money to make that place a reality. Thank you, Paul.

After Seattle, our next stop was Astoria. To arrive downtown, you drive over a big bridge that crosses the Columbia. We had chowder for lunch at a place that serves maybe the best chowder on the planet. If you're ever here, it's a tiny little place south of Commercial on 11th Street. We didn't stay too long. Mainly because we realized that between here and Pacific City, there was Cannon Beach. Down the 101 we drove. The tide was out when we got there. On the beach, we ran for a couple miles in both directions. That was fun. After a few days spent driving in a car, we were both ready to stretch the legs. At least I sure was.

It felt like we had the whole beach to ourselves. Though I could see how busy it must get in the warmer months. There's a tonne of hotels and motels and beachside B&B's and basically any type of accommodation you can think of. There were lots of dogs on the beach and I was happy to run around with them, have brief visits, learn more about what they had to say about rugged Oregon. Oregon's coast is rugged. I think that's what I like most about it. It's hilly, craggy, there's dense forest, big pieces of driftwood everywhere. At Cannon Beach, there are these huge rock spires perched in the sand.

Once we had our Cannon Beach fill, we continued on our way down to Pacific City. That it's called a city is a misnomer. It's tiny. There are like two or three restaurants here. I think there are more marijuana retailers than restaurants. The number of weed stores along the Oregon Coast is shocking. They are everywhere! And as promised, Meko continued the story of his trip with Sunny to Louisville. The Run For Roses. In my last letter, he left off when he and Sunny decided to go to Churchill Downs to place a big enough bet to buy back *Alysheba*. Between Seattle and Astoria and Pacific City, I was treated to the next part.

Yours Truly,
Foxworth

* * *

How Meko and Sunny arrived all the way to Tuscaloosa, Alabama after driving through places like Demopolis and Birmingham. And how the cousins discovered the eery Longstreet Plantation on the Mississippi Delta.

We were on the road first thing Monday morning. We didn't know where we'd stay for the night. We only knew that there were places in the Deep South we wanted to see. Both of us, having never been to this part of the country. Sunny found an Avis in the Ninth Ward of New Orleans and it was from that Avis our road trip began. Our chariot for the long drive north was a Ford Focus. Beautiful machine. It was everything we needed. The stereo could've been better, but oh well.

I was the first driver. Sunny's job while I drove was to reconfigure our flights. He's good at that stuff and had it all sorted out before we got to Baton Rouge. He was able to have our flights changed to credits for wherever our next flight would be. Of course, we didn't have an answer to that question, but at least we had the credits. As for our itinerary, we decided on no planning. We agreed that so long as we got to Churchill Downs before Saturday, it didn't matter what path we took.

Baton Rouge was boring. The most intriguing part of that area of Louisiana was the prisons and oil refineries along the road. There were several of each. The refineries are massive. And we had no idea what we were looking at. You look at these things and it's just a confusion of pipe and steel and smokestacks. After the cluster of refineries, we drove north on Highway 61. Inmates from nearby high security penitentiaries were busy with road work duties. It was kind of nerve wracking to be in such close vicinity to the inmates despite being in the comfort of our rented Focus. Who knows what those guys, and they were all guys, were doing time for? Of course, mass incarceration is an issue in the states and that was a point of discussion between Sunny and me. How many of these people working the roads in prison outfits should actually be there? Wrongful convictions occur a lot more often than we would like to think. And it's true, most of the guys working the roads were black. Again, if you were to read the major newspapers of record, you would be aware of how big an issue black Americans being unfairly targeted by the justice system is. How many of these guys, working the roads, without any of the freedom I think most people take for granted, deserved to be there? The Deep South is a place difficult to reconcile. There are really charming parts to it. And then of course, there is a horrible history of racial prejudice. Anyway, for this story, I won't say much more about that topic.

On the Focus' stereo, I told Sunny he had to play a playlist I made of Delta blues. After all, we were on the Blues Highway. It's a stretch of highway that goes as far as Greenville, Mississippi, north of Vicksburg. The Mississippi Delta is a place where the ghosts of slavery intermingle with the ghosts of Robert Johnson, Mississippi Fred McDowell, all those old blues greats. In the spring, it's wonderfully green and the roads were in good enough condition. It's a somnolent part of the country. Agrarian. Rolling hills. It was perfect setting for the blues I had Sunny play. Old stuff, the music that turned Keith and Mick and all the British blues guys on. Blues music is deceptively simple. It can be a simple as three chords over thirty-two bars, but with blues, less is more. The emotional depth of the music is clear and obvious.

We were listening to Fred McDowell for most of the drive north before reaching Natchez, Mississippi. We crossed into Mississippi from Louisiana about an hour north of Baton Rouge. McDowell plays a mean acoustic slide. All of his records sound like they were recorded on a creaky back porch overlooking the swampy delta in the middle of the night with a moon shining overhead partially obscured by clouds. There's a porch light flickering with bugs flying around it. It's reflective music. That's a McDowell record. Most of what he sang about, I have no real idea. I think context is everything and lord knows, I have minimal context about what really was going on in the days McDowell recorded. But it's good music.

Natchez is cute. It certainly caters to visitors. The town is situated on the shores of the Mississippi River. Boats big and small slowly cruised by the big ol' river as we drove around looking for a place for lunch. I asked Sunny if he wanted to go for a dip in the river. He declined. I went anyway. It was the best decision I made since deciding to go on this whole trip in the first place. Sunny, he doesn't like to move out of his comfort zone all that much. It's a quality that irks me because discomfort is a feeling I seek out. Healthy discomfort that is.

We had lunch at a cafe. The woman who served our coffee and sand-wiches wondered what had brought us to town. I told her we were "in search of the South." She laughed, I laughed, Sunny rolled his eyes. He ex-plained we were on our way to Kentucky for the Derby. She said she went there in the 1970s when she was in her twenties. She said that Hunter Thompson was right. As an event, it was decadent and depraved. "So of course, I had a hell of a good time," she said.

Sunny and I walked around Natchez with our coffees. There's not a whole lot to see. Well, that's what we thought until we found Smoot's. Smoot's is a grocery store, but it's more than that. It's also a place where musicians come to play. And it looks exactly as you would imagine a coun-try grocery store from the 1930s to look like. I ordered tamales. The old fella behind the counter took my money, which included a nice tip. He said, "Thanka suh." There's a slower pace in Mississippi.

Driving north along 61 from Natchez to Vicksburg, we found remnants of the South's Antebellum past. There were highway pullouts every so of-ten, and in those pullouts, there were plaques about some old bluesman. The Mississippi ran only a few miles to the west of the highway. Rich, fer-tile farmland surrounded us. Perpendicular to the road we travelled on were country roads leading into the lush forest toward the river.

Somewhere between Natchez and Vicksburg, I hung a left onto a dirt road that led to an old Antebellum estate. Down the road, we slowly drove. Not long was it before we were beneath a thick canopy of trees. Although there was a sign on the highway advertising the old mansion, Sunny and I weren't sure if the property welcomed visitors. The sign was old and faded and barely hanging on. Unlike the other signs we drove past that gleamed in the afternoon sun. We drove in anyway. It was the sign's poor condition that did it for me.

The further we drove toward the estate, the narrower the road became. I had to slow our rig down considerably. Must've been five miles before we reached what looked to be our destination. To our disappointment, we came upon a locked gate just as the old farmhouse came into view. On the rusted gate, there was a faded sign. It said: "Visitors Welcome." Sunny and I looked at the sign and then at each other.

"We should probably head back," I said.

"Head back? Really?"

"I don't know if this is the kind of place we want to see."

"Bullshit Meko, this is exactly your kinda place."

I was surprised at what Sunny was saying. He could probably see that I was a bit creeped out and that's enough fuel to egg that bastard on. So, we jumped the gate and proceeded in a direction toward the house.

Sunny: "You know what we should do?"

"What's that?"

"We should come back here at night."

"Oh yeah?"

"Yeah."

"Less than a couple hours ago, you wouldn't even jump in the river to cool off."

"Yeah well, when we were eating those tamales, I realized why we were on this trip in the first place."

"Von Rotz."

"Exactly."

I smiled and gave Sunny a shove. "You're crazy."

Down the road we walked. There was no sign of anyone living there. The big ol' plantation house, there it stood. Beautiful thing, really. Built probably in the 1850s in that iconic southern neo-classical Greco style. Big pillars, big balcony circumnavigating the whole house. This old plantation house was curiously pristine. Odd, why did the owners neglect the dilapidated highway sign, the rusted gates? When we got to to the front door, Sunny and I weren't sure if we should knock.

"Let's walk around back," I said.

"You see any cars or anything?"

"No, you?"

"You see that old farmhouse, I think they must park cars in that thing," Sunny said, pointing north.

A well worn path led from the main house where we stood to a big farmhouse about a kilometre away. We weren't exactly on the banks of the river, but we were close. Sunny said, "Maybe that's where a caretaker lives?"

"Must be."

Around the back, there was row after row of...it was hard to tell. Someone was preparing the soil for a crop. When I saw the prepped rows, I was convinced someone was living in the caretaker's house. Maybe he or she or that family happened to be in town. But then, it was such a huge property, they could be way out in the bush doing whatever one does on an old plantation on a spring Monday.

It was so quiet. That was another thing that creeped me out. Dead quiet all around save for the buzz of the occasional fly. On the back porch of the mansion, there was a sitting area. Sunny and I walked up to the rocking chairs set on either side of a coffee table. On the coffee table, there was an ashtray with newish looking cigarette butts. Looked like they'd been there not too long. I turned around to look toward the river. Sunny left the porch and started walking in that direction. Behind the chairs, there was a door. I put my hand on the knob and turned it. It wasn't locked. The door opened and there was another door. It too, wasn't locked.

I walked inside. My adrenaline was doing its thing. What did I see? It was dusty. There were old paintings on the wall. Looked like the place hadn't been lived in for quite some time. There were dusty black and white photos framed on hallway armoires. A staircase led up to the top level. I called out, "Hello? Anyone here?" No answer. At that point, did I turn around and return outside? No. I went further into the house. Through the rear hallway I walked, the floorboards creaking with every step I took. My breath, growing heavier with each step. A bead of sweat rolled down my right temple. Flies buzzed around my head. Maybe they could smell my anxiety.

I came upon the main living room. I tried calling Sunny's name, but he didn't respond. Must be out of earshot. The living room was grand. I walked over to the fireplace. Above the mantle, there was the massive head of a buck. Stuffed pheasants beautifully hung on each side of the fireplace. There were a few more framed pictures on the mantle. I picked one up and blew off the caked layer of dust. The photo was of a family gathering. Twenty odd people were lined up on the house's front porch. In the middle, there was a bride and groom. Of course, it was a wedding photo. I brought the picture closer, trying to examine the faces of those long since dead. Odd, no one was smiling. Everyone in the photo was white. The bride and groom, they looked terrific. A handsome pair. The groom was in a white tuxedo. It looked like it may have been a military suit. Was he a confederate? The bride's dress was huge and white and royal.

At the precise moment I returned the old photo back to the mantle, a door in the house slammed shut. I whirled around. A cloud had obscured the outside sun and so there was considerably less natural light in the room.

"Hello? Anyone there?" Nothing.

"Sunny? That you?" Nothing.

I took a few steps. The creaks in the floorboards, many decibels louder now than they were a few moments ago.

"Sunny? You there, man? Come on, cut it out."

Nothing. Fear gripped me. I rushed toward the nearest exit: the house's main front door. I turned the handle, it was locked. I fumbled around, trying to unlock the damn thing. I heard a floorboard creak behind me. I turned around. I practically yelled: "Who's there? Sunny?" Nothing. I ran toward the same door I came in at the back of the house. The door I had opened was now closed.

Sitting there was a cat. When it saw me, it started walking toward me. The cat brushed up against my leg. I bent down to try and pet it, but it ran away down the hallway in the direction I had just come from. No way was I going back there. I went out the back door to the back porch. The sun was no longer obscured by cloud. It shone down on me. I looked for Sunny. I couldn't see him anywhere. I called his name, there came no reply.

Far off in the distance, emerging from a downward rolling hill toward the river, I saw two figures walking toward me. I couldn't tell if one of them was Sunny. Slowly, they walked. Eventually, I could tell that yes, it was. The guy he was with walked with a cane. The guy had a considerable limp.

"Oh and here's Meko. Meko meet Chauncey, Chauncey meet Meko." I shook the black man's hand. Despite his old age, his frail frame, it was a handshake made of oak. I gave Sunny a quizzical look. He winked and mouthed "later."

"How do you do sir?" He didn't reply.

"Speak a little louder," Sunny said.

"HOW DO YOU..."

"Just fine boy, I can hear ya fine."

Sunny laughed.

Chauncey said, "That you in the haws I hear?"

"Well, er, yeah I was only for a second. You could hear me?"

"Naw, I just thought I heard uh door slam. Thas all. You see Missuh Longstreet?"

"Who?"

"Missuh Longstreet. Ownuh this here property suh."

"There's someone in there?"

"Ol' like me. Mussa been up top." I looked at Sunny. He had a wide grin.

"How old?"

"Missuh Longstreet, well he turn, let me think now, I turn eighty-eight last Septembuh...thank he a yeuh two ol'er than me...cain't really remembuh." Chauncey let go a laugh.

"And he's in there?"

Chauncey said nothing for a while. He looked over at the house, organized his thoughts.

"Maybe you saw some o' 'em photos in theyuh...Missuh Longstreet jes' a lil un in some uh them."

"I saw a wedding photo? Looked like it was a hundred years old."

"That'd be missuh's daddy's daddy, yeah thas what I think anyway," Chauncey said.

"Boys wan' drink or sompin'? Lemnade?"

"Thank you, but Meko and I, we should probably be on our way. We got a big drive ahead of us."

"Aw okay well, you boys, you come on back anytime now...okay?"

"Thank you Chauncey, and thank you for the tour of the property."

"Thas no problem son, no problem whassoeveh."

Sunny and I walked back to the car. As we drove back to the highway, we both demanded knowing what we each saw.

"You went in there? And you didn't see the old guy?"

"Sunny, there's no way someone is living in there. The whole house is caked with dust. Only thing I saw was an old cat."

"Yeah, but you heard Chauncey."

"Well of course."

"Maybe he meant Longstreet was the cat?"

"You really think? And did notice his eyes? They were kinda...cloudy?"

"Yeah I did...hey what's that flapping underneath the wiper?" Sunny spotted a folded piece of paper between the front windshield and the wiper.

"Pull over, see what it is."

"Nah I'll just slow down and reach out and grab it." After a brief struggle, with Sunny holding the wheel, I did exactly that and gave it to Sunny for him to read.

"Damn, this is nice handwriting."

"What's it say?"

"It's kinda hard to read this. You take a look." Sunny handed me the note.

"No trespassers, violators shot." Sunny and I looked at each other. We burst out laughing.

"What is this place?"

"Meko, let's get out of here!"

On the Blues Highway approaching Vicksburg, Sunny told me more about Chauncey. While I was in the house, he'd gone down to the river. He said he was splashing water in his face when he heard someone call from behind. Startled, he turned around and there was old Chauncey. Sunny said he had no idea the old man was anywhere in his vicinity. It was like he appeared out of thin air.

He asked a few questions with a stern look on his face and then, just as the sun went behind the cloud, the caretaker, if that's what he really was, went from stern to friendly and accommodating. He offered to walk Sunny around the property. Thoroughly freaked out, Sunny accepted the invitation. He asked Chauncey if they could start by walking toward the old house and that was when he saw me in the distance emerge from the house.

After I told him about what happened to me, the door slamming, the cat, we agreed that may well be one of the strangest experiences of our lives. I was driving, faster naturally. Instead of Mississippi Fred McDowell, I put on some Blind Willie Johnson. He has a song that we listened to more than once on that road trip. *Dark Was The Night, Cold Was The Ground.* That song, both Sunny and I agreed, was as haunting as our experience at Longstreet. Longstreet was the name we gave to that old plantation.

We didn't spend much time at all in Vicksburg. But we did in Jackson: Mississippi's state capital further to the east. In Jackson, we plotted out where we would end up for the night. Tuscaloosa, we figured, could be a good spot. Tuscaloosa is the home of the University of Alabama. A total college town, southern style. Roll Tide. I'd never seen the sort of campus life that exists at places like the University of Alabama. Neither had Sunny, who grew up in Canada. He was really into checking out the football stadium and those huge infamous Greek houses. So, over more tamales at a place called the Big Apple Inn in Jackson, Mississippi, we settled on where we would end up on day one of this road trip north through the Deep South.

What's a tamale, you may wonder? No, it's not those red candy's that you can buy in gas stations. An authentic tamale, like the ones we were devouring at this strange little place called the Big Apple Inn, is a traditional Mexican dish made with a corn based dough mixture filled with meats or beans and cheese. Tamales are wrapped and cooked in corn husks or banana leaves. They are removed from the husks before eating.

At Big Apple, ours were delicious. Why is that place odd? Well, it's this tiny little rundown restaurant that is one of the last remaining remnants of a time long since past in Jackson's history. Story goes, the Big Apple Inn used to be in the heart of a bustling Black American neighbourhood. A place where commerce happened, things were on the up and up and life was...good. At least as good as life could be for black people in a segregated south. This golden age of this former black neighbourhood in Jackson was a long time ago. Mid-century. Through the years, it gradually lost its identity and is now a far cry from what it once was. The Big Apple Inn is a reminder of what used to be. After all these years, it hasn't changed one iota. At least, I don't think it has. It's delicate territory for me, a white male, to try and give a cogent answer to the question of whether life has improved for black Americans. There are many race related issues that are very much alive in America today. But I think we've come a long way as well.

Sunny and I talked about Von Rotz on our approach to the Alabama border. The evening light fading as we drove. The topic of our discussion was, oddly, investing. See, Von Rotz was the first one to explain to us stocks and bonds. Back when we were little kids without the slightest clue about those sorts of things. While looking at the map of Tuscaloosa, I noticed that somewhat on our way was the town of Demopolis. Seeing Demopolis triggered a memory of a guy Von Rotz had made sure we read when both Sunny and I went through college. That man's name, Jim Rogers. Von Rotz had said to us that there were lots of lessons for us to learn about the world in Jim's writing. Jim, now in his late seventies, was born raised in Demopolis. Back then, there were so few people and it was so rural, that the Rogers house telephone number was five. That's it.

Rogers was an ace student and went to Yale first and then was a grad student at Oxford. Returning to the US, he got a job on Wall Street as an analyst. Eventually, at still a relatively young age, he started a hedge fund with a guy named George Soros. Rogers and Soros made big bucks betting on global financial events. They were the guys on the other side of the trade that nearly sank the Bank of England. It's complicated, but anyway, long story short, Rogers came from nothing, made a tremendous amount of money, and before he turned fifty, never had to work a day in his life again.

He manages his own money. He's written books - *Investment Biker* is his most well known. In that book, he travelled the globe on a motorbike, going to far flung places to explore and learn about different cultures and economies. Rogers is the kind of investor who looks under the rocks. He doesn't just look at digits flying across a ticker, no he wants to understand whether there's a hidden opportunity in a place like Namibia. The only way to know is to go there. Talk to the people, understand the place. See first hand developing markets. Developing markets are to Rogers the most exciting. They are also notoriously fickle. The rule of law is not ubiquitous around the world. Far from it. But with Rogers, I think he also just likes to travel and see new places. I can't blame him.

In fact, his official residence is now Singapore. Why Singapore? There's a reason. It's not just for the slings and the warm weather. Rogers famously has given up on the United States. He says America had its century, the 20th, England had its own, the 19th, and now the 21st belongs to Asia. If you were young and keen and smart, you moved to New York in the 20th century. London in the 19th, and Singapore in the 21st. Or any major city in Asia with close ties to China.

Rogers also likes to say that commodities are the best long term investment. Water and farmland, those kinds of commodities. Rogers believes that the pressures too many humans place on the planet inevitably will result in an insane demand for a finite supply of arable farmland. While his investment thesis has always made sense to me, just like it has for Von Rotz, there are problems. The main problem is timing. Yes, fresh, clean drinking water is very much a finite, precious resource, but what if it takes forty years before a meaningful return on playing that commodity as an investment?

In any event, Sunny and I, there we were driving our rented Focus from Mississippi toward Demopolis, Alabama, talking about Jim Rogers and global financial markets. We had Von Rotz to thank for introducing us to the Jim Rogers worldview. The Longstreet affair was in our rearview mirror. Our sights were set on exploring the unlikely hometown of a famous global investor. By the time we got there, it was dark and Sunny and I were ready for dinner. I think we had one of the best meals of the entire trip in Demopolis. The Red Barn, if you're ever in Demopolis, please go. It's far from fancy. It's the kind of place where the best qualities of rural southern hospitality sparkle. The portions are enormous. The prices are low. The food tastes otherworldly. And the scene, it's hard to describe. It's Alabama countryside. And I know it's easy to negatively associate the Alabama countryside with racial prejudice and all kinds of backward redneck thinking. Still, there is also a beautiful side to rural Alabama.

Let me try and explain. I'm sure the people dining that evening, without a cloud in the sky, full moon blazing, thought we were from Mars. But they were so friendly. Our waitress, Aunt Jemima herself, was exceedingly polite in telling us about Demopolis. She even gave us a few free dishes of food after she heard Sunny was from Canada. Her twenty-something son had just returned from a trip to Toronto for a Drake concert. He told his mom he loved Canada. She showered her goodwill on us. Thank you, Drake.

I had a big plate of mashed potatoes and gravy and roast beef and steamed veggies. I think Sunny had the same. It was magic. I think we spent nine bucks each on our meals. Thinking about that basic meal to this day makes my mouth water. With food, less is often more. Wafting through the air was a local rock n' roll station. Sunny and I, looking around the restaurant, were trying to understand where we were. Who were these people? What kinds of lives did they live down here? The quiet corners of America. This was the real deal. If we were in search of the South, we found a true chunk of it right there in the Red Barn. It was an experience I'll never forget.

On our way toward Tuscaloosa, we took an alternative route to get back to the interstate. Sunny was driving and I had us listening to an Alabama themed playlist. We were haulin' ass on this old road listening to Skynard's Free Bird turned way up. A giant Alabama full moon lit up the car's interior as if it were the sun itself. The sky was completely clear, the stars were out, it was warm, no wind...so alive!

In town, it didn't take long for us to find a motel. The one we found was right in the heart of Tuscaloosa. It was past midnight when we checked in. The front desk manager told us about what town was like on game day.

For football, that is. He said it was near impossible to find a room anywhere in the county. Room rates went through the roof. This occurred every single time there was a home game. Every single time. The stadium turned into a complete crimson tide madhouse. Tickets to the games were also near impossible to find. Even students had a hard time tracking down spare tickets. There is nothing remotely like this where I grew up. Neither for where Sunny grew up in Alberta. In our spartan motel, both of us were long gone to the land of nod in no time.

In the morning I went for a run. I wanted to explore Tuscaloosa and the University of Alabama campus on foot. Running, an old standby for me to explore new territory. I was up surprisingly early, around six-thirty. Sunny showed no signs of life. If, first thing in the morning, going for a run is not what the mind or body wants, the most challenging part of the process isn't the part where you do the actual activity. No, the hardest part is putting the running shoes on, bending down and tying them up. The shoe hurdle was alive and well that morning. But I overcame and soon found myself taking in, running through, the early morning Alabama air in a place called Tuscaloosa. It was the first of May. If the student body wasn't done with their exams already, whoever was left would soon be. At Dartmouth, I never went past the third week of April for my exams and as soon as that day came, I was out of there, on the road, see you in September New Hampshire.

On the University of Alabama campus, I saw far more students than anticipated. Perhaps the most striking observation I made was what they, the girls, all wore. Seemed like every girl on campus wore the same outfit. Long, baggy, white t-shirts that went as far as halfway down the thigh. I was too shy to ask why.

The campus is huge. And the buildings are old and beautiful. The main boulevard has these big trees lining it the entire way through the heart of campus. The Black Warrior River runs adjacent. I went down to the brown river and ran through a riverside green space all the way back toward town as far as the public library and then returned to campus. I ran past the stadium, which at that hour in the morning was lifeless. I ran past all the frat and sorority houses. Those old neo-classical revival houses are massive. When I was in college, I actively avoided Greek life. I never understood the draw. You pay big bucks to join a club that you have to try-out for at the start of your freshman year. Everyone talks about how great frat parties are, how great the social life is. At least where I was in Hanover, I just couldn't get past the phoniness of the whole thing.

I once had a friend who rushed. His subscription to Greek Life became a wedge in our former friendship. When I first met Bob in the first week of our first year of university, I saw a brainy science major with a long curly ponytail and a penchant for wearing ratty old housecoats. In our dorm rooms, we were only allowed hot plates. Bob was in his room cooking lentils, grinding free trade, organic coffee beans, doing all these things that spoke of his Oregon roots. And he kept referring to a guy back home called Boom. Eventually, we learned that was what he called his dad. Flash forward to the final party of that crazy first year of university. Boom was there and he rolled the biggest joint I still have ever seen. Back home in Portland, Boom works as an ACLU lawyer. Apparently, he's an Oregon legend. Bob and I were in a few classes together. We often played our guitars for the rest of the people on our floor after far too much cheap beer. For some strange reason, Bob felt a pull toward joining a fraternity. He rushed, pledged, or whatever the process is, and when he was selected, from then on, he slowly just...changed. He cut his hair, wore cleaner clothes, never really hung out on our floor anymore. The life, the joie de vivre, it was sucked out of him. He became clubby and secretive. It was tragic.

What I was seeing as I ran past sorority after sorority house were groups of gorgeous girls. And they were doing things like mowing the front lawn, hanging laundry, throwing frisbees around, playing cards on the front steps of the house. I stopped at, I think it was Alpha Omega Delta, or maybe it was Alpha Omega Epsilon, or maybe it was Gamma Phi Beta, whichever one it was, and I asked a girl playing the violin next to an open fluid dynamics textbook what her sorority was all about. She recited to me while playing her Strauss the following:

"We promote ideals and objectives to help further the advancement of female engineers and technical scientists, while at the same time encouraging bonds of lifelong friendships among members.

We value friendship, leadership, and professionalism. Friendship lies at the heart of every activity in which our members participate. Leadership opportunities at the chapter and international levels are available to members. Professionalism is integral to promoting the purpose of our sorority and we are dedicated to educating the community on the importance of women in technical fields and encouraging young women to pursue technical careers. For more information, visit our website at..."

When she was done talking, she looked up at me, without skipping a beat in the etude she was masterfully playing. She stared deep into my soul and smiled. The morning sun hit her golden hair and golden face perfectly. I ran.

Sunny was up and ready to get some breakfast when I returned to the motel. After I told him about my run, about the girl at Gamma Delta Zeta, or Omega Epsilon Phi, or whatever it was, he said that was the kind of girl for him. At the time, Sunny was on a break from a long time girlfriend. Perplexed, I asked why. "I need structure," he said. There was nothing else I could think to do but shake my head, roll my eyes. Sunny and I are similar in many ways but also very different.

We drove through campus and went to the central cafe. Over our coffees and eggs and toast, we discussed our next move. Where would we end up tonight? It was an open question. Sunny found a state map in the motel's lobby that included Georgia and Tennessee. It was Tuesday. We had the rest of today and three more days before the fateful Derby. Between where we sat in Tuscaloosa and Louisville, there was lots of terrain. Birmingham was a short drive away, and so was Montgomery. Sunny and I agreed we wanted to see Memphis, which was in our general direction headed north.

Sunny: "So, you wanna just end up in Memphis tonight?"

"We could, or we could spend more time in Alabama and head up to Hunstville or something. That's where they did a lot of the early work for the space program."

"Really?"

"Yeah, I read about it a few years ago. German rocket scientists fled Europe during the second world war and ended up in the states. The government put them to work in places like Huntsville."

"What book was that?"

"Space, by Michener. I thought you read him?"

"No. Too long."

"Would you want to see Huntsville?"

"To be honest, not really."

"Fair enough. So then straight to Memphis?"

"If we go to Memphis tonight, then where would you want to go after?"

"Nashville, I guess? For a couple nights there or a couple nights in Memphis?"

"I definitely want to go to those places. See Beale Street and Broadway."

"Yeah me too. But what about Atlanta?"

"Isn't that too far?"

"No, I think it would only be another couple hours driving from Birmingham."

"Atlanta would be cool."

"Okay, so should we try and get to Atlanta?"

"I mean, that works for me. I have no real idea what to do in Atlanta, or what to see but...why not?"

"Okay, then. Atlanta it is! And then, from there, we can maybe swing back through Birmingham to end up in Memphis? I don't know, let's not get ahead of ourselves."

"Agreed. That's not the way we want to do this trip."

"I wonder how Von Rotz is doing anyway?"

"I've been thinking a lot about him."

"How so?"

"Come on, let's go walk around campus. I'll tell you while we walk. We got another big day of driving ahead of us and I want to experience some roll tide."

As we ambled our way through campus, Sunny told me about the time Von Rotz took us for one of our first sailing trips. It's a good story, so I'll repeat it here for you.

Having never before sailed, Von Rotz put us to work immediately upon our arrival at the dock. At the time, he was mooring *Alysheba* in Vancouver harbour up in British Columbia. It was the summer after we graduated from university. This trip, from Vancouver up to the northernmost tip of Vancouver Island and back, it was his present to us.

We brought along girlfriends and he had friends joining us as well. It was a full boat and the weather was peak summer, mid-July. Sunny and I were keen to learn how to sail. And in Von Rotz, we had a willing instruc-tor. On day one, we went across the Strait of Georgia and overnighted on Galiano Island, a beautiful little island on the outer reaches of the southern gulf islands. There are few services on Galiano.

Since we would be spending a few nights on Salt Spring before sailing north, we didn't have any food on the boat for that first night on Galiano. That was Von Rotzian logic. He said that if we wanted to eat that night, we would need to catch our food. We were all starving. It was a rude surprise to us after the five hour trip across the Strait. Anyway, that was what we ended up having to do that first night. We hunted for our dinner and breakfast on Galiano Island.

The hunting party consisted of Sunny, myself, our girlfriends Ana and Melissa, Von Rotz, and his two friends Sue and Rog. We huddled on the shore with beers and glasses of wine in hand to hash out our plan. We approached it with the seriousness of a coordinated campaign. Von Rotz gave us the rundown on the boat's available weaponry. We had three shotguns, six fishing rods, two daggers, and a mallet. The big steel mallet with a rubber handle, we weren't sure what that could be used for. Von Rotz saw our puzzled looks and said, "for the death blows."

Sunny and his girl Ana took a shotgun and a dagger. Melissa and I each grabbed a shotgun. The others took the rest. We fanned out. We were moored near the northern tip of the island. Up there, Von Rotz knew a landowner that had given his blessing for us to hunt on his land. We started our hunt at dusk. We agreed to bring our kill back to the boat before midnight. Midnight sharp would be when the cookout started. Our available food supply was mainly just deer. There wasn't enough space in the forest to hunt for bird. Rog and Sue took a rowboat out in a little bay to look for crab and fish. I have no clue where Von Rotz went. Sunny and Ana went to the south and Melissa and I turned north when we hit land. Melissa and I spread out, but then she called me and said that she wouldn't want to shoot anything, having never done it before.

Galiano has a deer problem. They are everywhere. There are no natural predators. The natural ones, the wolves and cougars, have been extirpated. It was dark before we knew it. Two hours in, I hear a shot and Sunny yell. "I hit one!" That was all Melissa and I heard. We gave ourselves another hour before deciding hunting wasn't for us. Back at the boat, Von Rotz was there with the rest. The only other success was Rog. He pulled in six crab. Sunny and I dragged the deer across a grassy two-track trail as Von Rotz led us to his friend's place. I had no idea where we were going. I don't think anyone did. Not even Von Rotz, despite him giving the impression that he knew exactly where we were at all times.

It was half past one in the morning once we located Spalding's. Spalding, an old friend of Von Rotz, was the owner of this old hunting cabin in the Galiano Island backwoods. It was a true hunting cabin. Spalding was tending the fire when we trampled in through the backdoor. He said he thought we'd never make it and then asked Von Rotz for the kill. I brought Spalding outside and showed him the dead animal. He got me to help him drag the thing behind the cabin and we hung it up on a hook he'd fastened to a sturdy cedar. Spalding led me back to the house. I was confused about what we were going to end up doing for dinner. He led me through a different door into the kitchen and there I saw this massive feast he was almost done preparing for us. He needed my help bringing the food out. He had a couple big roasts, platters of sides, bottles of wine, and bread loaves. He and Von Rotz had this planned the entire time. I learned later the deer was our token of gratitude.

Not since then have either of us gone on a hunt. In Tuscaloosa, Alabama, our retelling of that memory momentarily had us reconsider our plans. I asked Sunny if he wanted to find an outfitter and hunt in the Alabama wilderness. He laughed. To actually go on a hunt would take money and luck. We agreed that a trip like that would be for another time.

"Let's go on a different kind of hunt," Sunny said.

"What kind are you thinking?"

"Why don't we go back to the car and begin again our odyssey through the paved wilderness."

"Nothing else you want to see?"

"I'm good, actually let me find myself a hat for the sun."

In a Crimson Tide gift shop, Sunny tried on a few different ball caps. Shopping for a hat had us discussing our Derby outfits. Neither of us had anything suitable to wear for Saturday's big event. Of course, we didn't exactly know what suitable actually was, but we had an idea forged from some distant Kentucky Derby cliche. Light blues, whites, rose coloured suits and fedoras. The southern gentleman look.

"Why don't we look for those kinds of clothes once we get to Louisville," I said as Sunny paid up.

"If we get there Friday night, we can go then, or I guess we could also go before on Saturday morning."

"All I think we really need is a couple blazers, a button-up and some shoes."

"And a bow tie," Sunny said.

"You want a bow tie, go right ahead. Maybe I'll get a cigar."

"Oh, I'm gettin' a cigar that's for damn sure, maybe one of them Panama hats too."

Sunny drove us from Tuscaloosa to Birmingham. Talk of Derby clothes naturally progressed to other important matters like our gambling strategy. We were both clueless. Neither of us had ever been to a horse race, let alone figured out the right kinds of bets. As soon as we started talking about betting, Sunny pulled over and asked if I could drive. He wanted to use the time to teach himself how to bet at the Derby, having only then realized how inept we were. Betting isn't my interest or forte, so I was glad when he volunteered to take that job on. I'm better at driving. I exited off the I-20 to find us some country roads. I get so sick of interstate driving. It bores me to tears.

We drove east on the 216 toward Birmingham. Sunny was scrolling his phone, lost in trying to give himself a crash course on giving us the best chance to make money. The amount of money we figured we'd need to win was two-hundred grand. To us, a fortune. Between the two of us, we were able to scrounge up ten grand for our stake. I had no clue if our goal was realistic. But Sunny kept finding article after article about people winning lots of money from bets of less than twenty bucks. At the last Derby, a woman won $1.2 million on a $17 bet. I almost drove off the road when Sunny told me that. How was that even possible? I wasn't aware that you can structure a bet in the Kentucky Derby however way you want. What she did was make a simple "pick five" wager. She got extremely lucky that each horse she chose to win actually won. See, on race day, there are lots of different races throughout the day that lead up to the actual run for the roses. She selected the correct winners for each race. Had one of her picks not won, no bueno.

Sunny came across tonnes of other clever betting systems and techniques. If you scratch the internet's surface, quickly you realize how much information there is out there on the interwebs. It's overwhelming to have the history of information at our fingertips. I figured the only way we'd have a reasonable shot at winning the boat money would be to use up our ten grand with a bunch of smaller bets rather than a few big bets. Sunny thought the other way around. He believed in concentrating our portfolio in no more than five bets. This disagreement was the root of our first big argument on the trip. We didn't have many, but when we did, they were volcanic. We weren't speaking on our approach to Birmingham. The only one speaking was Jim James on the stereo. My Morning Jacket's latest record was the only thing we could agree to listen to.

At the Alabama capitol building, I stretched out on the front lawn. Eyes closed, breezy, I gave in. I yelled out to Sunny, who was walking up the building's massive stone staircase. "Fine, we'll do it your way!"

"You won't be sorry!"

That was all he had to say.

* * *

I wrote all of that last night while Meko was out for dinner here in Pacific City. He must've gone for a walk or a run or something because he was gone for a really long time. This morning I got up early to finish off what I wanted to tell you about Oregon before driving south.

Today, we will try and get as far as Coos Bay, which is only a threeish hour drive south. I forgot to say that when we drove through Cannon Beach, there was an old movie theatre along the 101 that was playing Robert Redford's supposed last movie before retiring. *The Old Man and the Gun.* What a sight. A small town on the Oregon Coast. A midcentury single screen theatre complete with the rows of bulbs and the outwardly projected triangular shaped marquee. And on that marquee in big bold capital letters: *THE OLD MAN AND THE GUN* - above that in even bigger letters: *REDFORD.* Do they make movie stars like Redford anymore? Like Newman? I'm skeptical.

When Meko saw that theatre, he mentioned for the first time more of our future plans. When he saw that it was a Redford movie, he turned and said: "Maybe we'll see him in Park City." He meant that on our drive home from San Francisco, we were going through the Rocky Mountains. Park City was on our itinerary, as was Tahoe, Aspen, and then south to Taos.

I couldn't believe what I was hearing. Only then did Meko tell me that this trip was for his work. He had a friend in Aspen he needed to visit. The reason we were going to the Bay Area was for him to meet with people to report a different story. Meko is trying to be a freelance journalist right now and his life is a never ending hustle from one story, publication, interview to the next. It's the opposite of the kind of stable ranch work that Meko said Sunny prefers. At least I get to go to all these different places.

NOVEMBER 4

Dear Lula Mae,

Greetings from California! In one day, we made it as far south as Eureka from our Pacific City surfside motel. I write this to you from yet another motel in Eureka's Old Town. It's nearing midnight. I have quite a bit to fill you in on. We left Pacific City after a short, early morning jog along the beach. We ran and we got sprayed a few times from the splashing ocean waves. The weather worsened overnight and just as we got in the car to start our southern drive along 101, the skies opened up. Big time rains. The kind of rains we knew would eventually hit us by virtue of spending a few days in the Pacific Northwest.

I don't need cloudless skies to appreciate the landscapes in front of me. In fact, I was charmed by the heavy coastal rains we had all the way to Dunes City. The rain and the wind and the grey skies juxtaposed nicely with the thick evergreen forests we drove alongside and sometimes through. As I've said in a previous letter, Oregon is rugged. It's rough and tumble. It's clearly not as prosperous as Washington to the north, California to the south. This is precisely why I have come to like Oregon so much. There's plenty of logging. Lumber yards, mills, trucks, they are everywhere one looks. I'm glad we stuck to the coast. Meko was tempted to drive east through Portland and Eugene but, no, he decided we would stay on the 101 from Astoria all the way to San Francisco. Slow and windy, it's the best kind of road trip.

All of the little towns and communities we drove through had attractive qualities. Lincoln City, Depoe Bay, Otter Rock, Newport, Seal Rock,

Waldport, Yachats, Florence, Dunes City and Reedsport. The stretch of coastline between Newport and Florence, simply stunning. After Reedsport came Coos Bay. In Coos Bay, we had our lunch and went for a walk. Meko said that aside from being a mill town, Coos Bay was notable for another reason: Steve Prefontaine. He was born there. There is a giant mural on the side of a brick building with his painted image right in the heart of downtown. There on the side of that wall, Pre lives on. Do you know his story?

His dad was a welder, his mom a seamstress. Pre was working class Oregon.

Born in 1951, Pre ascended from hometown Coos Bay hero to record-setting college phenomenon, to internationally acclaimed track star. He was that rare combination of drive, work ethic and natural talent. He never lost a race in the three mile, 5,000 metre, six mile, or 10,000 metre events in his four years at the University of Oregon. His coach was the legendary Bill Bowerman, an icon in his own right. Bowerman helped a young accountant, one of his former runners, start a business of selling Japanese imported running shoes. They called their venture Blue Ribbon Sports. Eventually, the name was changed to Nike. I could tell you more about Bowerman, but that's for another time. Pre was famously known as an aggressive front runner. He'd go out hard from the start, claim the lead and did everything he could to never let anyone run in front. A couple of years after he finished college, after going to the Munich Olympics, Pre was killed in a car accident. He was returning to his Eugene home from a party after winning a 5,000 metre race. He drove off the side of the road to avoid oncoming traffic. He was twenty-four years old. There is a memorial at the base of the roadside boulder where he died. They call it Pre's Rock. It reads:

"Pre"

For your dedication and loyalty
To your principles and beliefs...
For your love, warmth, and friendship
For your family and friends...
You are missed by so many
And you will never be forgotten...

At the time of his death, Pre was considered the most popular athlete in Oregon. Along with a few other runners of his time, he was credited with sparking the national running boom of the 1970s. He's since been rightly deified. Hollywood has made movies about him. Meko was inspired by the mural of Pre. We went for a run through the Coos Bay streets. Although Oregon has a rough charm, there is a darker side. Running through town, it was shocking to see the number of homeless.

Meko went into a store and returned with a few documents that he said I needed to read tonight. I made sure to read them before writing this letter to you. The papers are notes from a speech Pre made at a big banquet in 1974. Far as I'm concerned, they should be required reading for anyone. I'll summarize the notes for you here:

What does cross-country do for the athlete?

A) *It builds toughness both mentally and physically.*
B) *Character - You have to be a special breed of cat to get up at five or six in the morning for that workout.*
C) *Builds Pride - When you succeed in a tough workout or race, you feel good about it and you should.*

D) *Dedication - You have to be dedicated because you're the only person that can do the work. No one else can do it for you.*
E) *Friendship - The guys you workout with have a very common bond and interest. All of you can relate to the work you have done and have to do.*

Cross-country Training and Racing

As an individual and as a team, know your competition, know the course and practice for the race.

Cross-country in the United States

As a sport, it's a team sport of individuals.

A) *The total score is important. The number five man is just as important as the number one man.*
B) *Each man competes against his self and that way he helps the team.*

Three Key Factors to Successful Running

1) *Diet*
2) *Rest*
3) *Training*

All must be consistent.

My favourite is his three key factors. Wonderfully simple. Pre is a hero to many and for good reason. Guys like him don't come around too often. Diet, rest and training. You could apply that to anything! Anyway I can't say enough about the rugged beauty of the Oregon Coast. South from

Coos Bay, there's Port Orford, Ophir, Nesika Beach, Gold Beach and the final town before the California frontier: Brookings. I got goosebumps when we crossed from Oregon into golden California. The skies had cleared and the evening sun was magnificent as it slowly approached the western horizon. Pink and purple and orange and everything in between. The road we travelled along, the 101, was in noticeably better condition as soon as we crossed into California. Also, Meko, who as you may know, has a history of speeding, thus far in our trip only received one speeder.

The flashing lights appeared in the rearview south of Carpenterville before we got to Brookings. Meko was travelling eighty in a sixty zone. The road patrol gave him the ticket and said we'd receive the actual fine in the mail. We didn't know how much the penalty would end up being. Meko was not happy about it. The cop could tell. He said, "Better here than in California. Consider me doing you a favour."

"How so?" Meko asked.

"The state of California is so far in debt, they've raised fines. This ticket I'm giving you will cost no more than two hundred. Down in California, same infraction, you're looking at triple."

Meko stopped for gas in Crescent City, the northernmost town on the California coast. Of course, the gas was more expensive than in Oregon. Gas prices, speeder prices, I was already getting a sense that California isn't a place they give away.

So, that pretty well brings you up to speed on how we got to Eureka before the sun was completely down. Initial impressions of Old Town Eureka: I like it here. So lush and fresh and green and the air is warm and inviting. We got lucky because there happened to be a midweek farmer's market, arts and craft bazaar going on tonight. One of the vendors said this county-wide event only happens once per month!

From store to store, booth to booth, gallery to gallery, we walked around among the Humboldt County locals. Humboldt County is famous for its Redwoods, but I was surprised to also be informed that it is a national leader in weed production. Again, like the Oregon coast, pot store after pot store line the streets of Eureka. They are everywhere.

Everyone was friendly. We stopped for dinner at cafe type restaurant and we ate well. I had my usual that Meko gave me and he had hamburgers and beer. Meko had a chat with our waitress about town. She said it was a nice place, but it wasn't without its problems.

"Drugs, mainly," she said.

"What kinds?"

"Hard stuff. Fentanyl, opioids, meth. There's a stretch of town heading south before Wabash Ave that everyone calls meth row."

"Meth row?"

"The state, the county, they're trying to address the issue, but it's far from an easy one to sort out as you can imagine."

After our dinner, Meko led us to a few art galleries. To be expected, the paintings were mostly coastal or redwoods landscapes. Acrylics and oils and a few silkscreens. The pottery was terrific. Though Meko wasn't too impressed. He wanted live music and it was at that point he dropped me off at our little motel. He said he'd be back in a little while. Well, it's now approaching one in the morning, no sign. We had almost eight hours in the car today, so you better believe I got another big piece of Run For Roses. I'll record that down now before I get too sleepy and forget the details. I must say, after hearing this latest installment, I would love to take a trip to Atlanta.

Xoxox
Foxworth

* * *

How the cousins discovered the healing powers of Waffle House, the ap-petite for blues on Edgewood Ave and how Meko's first encounter went with the enigmatic mystical Sam Decker of Tassajara Racing.

Maybe it was because we were in a rush to get to Atlanta. Maybe it was because of the argument that I eventually conceded to Sunny. Maybe it was neither of those things. Either way, we didn't find Birmingham at all inter-esting. Of course, any new place has interesting aspects, but in Birming-ham, we found nothing save for the noble capitol. I think there's more going on in Montgomery - ground zero for lots of the civil rights memori-als. We didn't have time to get there, so we just saddled up and drove east toward Hot 'Lanta.

Right about where you turn off the interstate to drive south to Tal-ladega, Sunny pulled over for gas. After going in to pay, I said to him the coolness that was still present between us needed to go. The trip wouldn't work otherwise. It was as simple as voicing my thoughts. In an instant, it was like nothing happened between us. To confront is to move forward. Just like that, we were freewheelin'. We considered going to Talladega to check out the NASCAR speedway, but there wasn't enough time if we wanted to arrive in Atlanta before dark. Maybe on the way back through to Memphis we would give our greetings to Ricky Bobby.

We took the I-20 into Atlanta. The traffic going west out of the city on that major highway, which sometimes is six lanes wide, was bumper to bumper. Thus far, of the cities encountered on our trip, New Orleans we found to be large, Birmingham moderately sized, Jackson, lesser so than Birmingham. Atlanta is a massive city. It's a sprawling metropolis that stretches far and wide across the Georgia landscape. People are everywhere. There's a vast downtown with plenty of high rises. But the bulk of the city is found outside of the central business district.

For Sunny and I, it was overwhelming. We had no idea where to go, what to do, where to stay. Sunny meanwhile wasn't feeling too hot on our approach to the city. Crossing the Chattahoochee into a western suburb, he was complaining about not feeling great at all. I turned off my music to tune into the local Atlanta radio. There was news on and it had to do with the forthcoming midterm elections. Sunny was moaning and groaning like John Lee Hooker. He was writhing in pain as I tried taking in what the pollsters were predicting. I asked him what was wrong and he said he didn't know. I asked him if he felt like it was the flu or a cold, he said he didn't think so. I asked him if he thought it was something he ate, he said he wasn't sure.

"What was the last thing you ate?"

"Well the last big thing I ate was the meal we shared at the McDonalds in Birmingham." It couldn't have been that since I was feeling fine.

"There's nothing else you've eaten?"

"Only this," he said. He had a bag of salted peanuts purchased from the gas station near Talladega.

"Let me see that." Sunny had polished the whole bag off. I looked at it, then I looked at him. He knew and I knew it had to be the peanuts.

"You ate the whole bag?

"Yeah, salted peanuts, once you start it's hard to stop."

I looked at the nutritional information. This bag of peanuts was a nutritional holocaust. The serving size on the bag was listed as one-tenth. A few quick mental calculations, one-tenth I figured would equal about fifteen peanuts. One-tenth of the bag had a quarter of the recommended daily intake of sodium. Sunny therefore had an astronomical amount of salt in his system from that one bag of peanuts alone. And the McDonald's didn't help.

"Look at this!"

"Look at what?"

"You know how much salt you ate?"

"It's just peanuts." I showed him the back of the label.

"Oh," he said. His complexion was pale, there was a bead of sweat running down his left temple. His face looked bloated. It was brine soaked crawfish all over again.

In New Orleans, I bought us a big tub of crawfish to eat as we walked from Jazz Fest back to the city. There's a particular way to eat those mudbugs. You have to crack them and then slurp up their meaty tails. The brine those street mudbugs are soaked in brings the salt levels to incredible highs. The day after the crawfish and all the other salty foods eaten in New Orleans, our ankles were completely swollen. My ankles looked as though I rolled both of them on both sides several times.

At first, as you can imagine, we were alarmed. Neither of us had experienced this before. One of our dorm room roommates asked us what we'd eaten. I told him about the mudbugs and he said: "You've eaten too much salt. Drink water. Lots of it." So, we did. I drank seven gallons that last day in New Orleans. Sunny had eight. The eighth gallon was meant to demonstrate he could drink more water than me. Sunny and I have little unvoiced competitions going all the time.

In the car ride into Atlanta, there was now a new competition. How quickly could I get us to a hotel to check-in without having to exit off the interstate? Exiting off the interstate was not going to happen. Doing so would force us into the crucible of the masses trying to flee the city back to their suburban dwellings. There was a tidal wave of traffic driving in our opposite direction.

I kept looking over at Sunny. He was having a nasty reaction to the salts in his blood. One moment he would feel extremely nauseous. The next, he would see things outside in those tall Georgian pines. "Look!" He'd say. "There's a giant peach over there! A big giant Georgia peach!" Knowing full well that there was no giant Georgian peach to see, I nonetheless would look over to humour his delirium. I did feel traces of guilt for not pulling over to a passing gas station for water. But we needed to get to our hotel.

"Be useful!" I said, after losing my patience. For the fifth time in twenty minutes, he claimed to see a giant peach.

"Find us a cheap hotel in a good part of town. Focus, Sunny. Focus!"

"Meko, I will do all that I can," he said gallantly.

The assignment of work to my ailing companion did the trick. Sunny found us a Marriott near Centennial Olympic Park. On TripAdvisor, the hotel had two stars. Good enough for us.

Sunny agreed to all sorts of things as he clicked his way through the hotel's third party booking agent to get us a room for eighty bucks. He said his email in no time at all was being bombarded by junk mail. Penis enlargement, medicare providers, survey all-stars, all kinds of junk. But we had our cheap room.

Shaunice at the concierge desk was angelic. She saw the poor condition of my cousin and she gave us an immediate, localized prescription. She said we needed to go to a Waffle House. She said, "Ain't nothin' Waffle House can't fix." Waffle Houses, ubiquitous through the south, are apparently the place to go to combat excessive sodium intake. "Happens all the time," she said. I looked at her like, really? "Trust me." She handed me a five dollar coupon.

There was a Waffle House across the street from the hotel. It was half past five when Shaunice dragged Sunny into that eating establishment. Shaunice said she would look after swollen clammy Sunny while I took our bags up to the thirtieth floor of this hotel high rise.

Through the doors, I walked and into the fluorescent interior of the fabled Waffle House. Shaunice had poor Sunny propped up in a corner booth. His right arm over her shoulders. His face, ghostly white, puffed up. His eyes, bloodshot and cloudy.

Shaunice was reading to Sunny verse from her new testament in a hushed voice. "He will wipe away every tear from their eyes, and death shall be no more, neither shall there be mourning, nor crying, nor pain anymore, for the former things have passed away. And he who was seated on the throne said, 'Behold, I am making all things new.' Amen." After Shaunice finished her reading, she turned to look at me. "Revelation 21:4-5," she said solemnly. Shaunice promised that if I ordered off the main menu a unique dish using special jargon, Sunny's problems would be gone in less than eight minutes provided the entirety of the prescription was ingested. She whispered into my ear specific instructions and then sent us off. "God-speed," she said.

I went up to the counter on a mission. The employee behind the counter warmly greeted me.

"Welcome to Waffle House sir, what can I git for ya?"

"Hi, I have an order that I've been told I need to whisper."

"Pardon me, sir?"

"I have a special request. It's for my ailing cousin."

"You want a waffle, or?" Leaning over the counter, I tried to whisper the order, but the lady moved backward.

"Sir, just tell me what you want. You don't need to whisper anything." Distraught, I looked over to where Shaunice and Sunny sat. Shaunice was nodding at me as if to say, go on, do as I said. I turned back around. Standing in front of me was Dustin, the manager.

"Here, I have this coupon for five bucks and I'd like to make a special order."

"Sir, have you been harassing Mia here?"

"No sir, I haven't."

"That's what she told me."

"No sir, I assure you I haven't."

"All right, gimme that coupon. What do you want to order." What more could I do other than settle on loudly whispering? I loudly whispered across the counter for an All-Star Breakfast and then, as per Shaunice's instructions, I winked my left eye twice and smiled a big smile, eyes ablaze.

Like clockwork, Dustin's eyes lit up, he tilted his head back, and then he looked at me as if there was one last thing I needed to say before he proceeded with the order.

In a true whisper, I said: "Cook that shit up, Quay." Dustin looked at me as if to say: "Who do you know?" Immediately, the look on his face changed from condescending authority to one of utmost respect and reverence. I said nothing more. Moments later, the meal was presented.

"Sir, that will be seven," Dustin said.

"Seven?"

"I, I, I...meant to say five. Five sir, five dollars even."

"That will do." I produced from my wallet a crisp five note. Before I turned to take the blessed All-Start Breakfast, Dustin and Mia and the rest of the staff in that Waffle House closed their eyes and crossed themselves.

Holding the tray of food, I turned around to walk to Sunny's table. There Sunny was sprawled out in the booth. Shaunice, however, was gone. She'd vanished. "Sunny, what happened to Shaunice?"

"Who?"

"Shaunice!"

"Who? Meko that you? Where are we?"

"Sunny, sit up! I have your medicine. You have to eat everything on this tray if you want to have any hope."

"Who's Shaunice?" Sunny was losing it. I placed the tray on the table in front of us and then propped him up with all my strength. The strength of a thousand men. His face was a disturbing mix of white and blue. His eyes looked like they both were afflicted with severe pink eye. He was breathing heavily, he was feverish, he was on the precipice of complete internal annihilation.

"Here! Eat this!" I cried, as I lifted toward his mouth a plastic forkful of syrupy waffle. Reluctantly, he slowly opened his mouth. I force fed him the fork-full and helped moved his jaw up and down with my hands to initiate the mastication process. Minutes later, he swallowed that first fateful bite. It felt like hours had gone by for that one measly bite. And there was still a mountain of food in front of him. But lord have mercy! That one bite of food, it made all the difference. The dream came true! At once, his face returned to a semi-normal colour. The sweats stopped, his pink eyes whitened, and the bloating was all but gone. And was that a smirk? Was that a little laugh I heard? Each bite went down smoother, easier and quicker than the last. In fifteen minutes, the entire tray of food was gone. And Sunny, he had a bright aura of light shine around his body like he was a gift from Him above.

The dream came true! Can I get a witness? Shaunice was right! Lord have mercy! Sunny looked at me. He was Adonis. Right there, in that Atlanta Waffle House, I was seated next to a Greek God. Sunny looked at me. His face was golden, his hair was golden. His eyes were a perfect blue. His smile was a million watts. He may as well have been Zeus himself. He looked at me and he said: "And now my head shall be lifted up above my enemies all around me, and I will offer in his tent sacrifices with shouts of joy; I will sing and make melody to the Lord."

We left the Waffle House after Sunny took a quick bathroom break. I was waiting for him outside. Through the doors he walked. I couldn't believe my eyes. What had happened to Adonis? It was Sunny, plain old Sundance Kid. He'd returned to earth in his former shell like nothing ever happened. Looking around him, stretching his arms, cracking his back, yawning a sweet yawn, Sunny, who may as well have just woken from fourteen hours of deep restorative sleep said, "Where to next?"

"No idea." I was envious of his condition. Where was Shaunice when we needed her? When I needed her? Shaunice would know where to go in Atlanta on a Tuesday night. "Let's go see if she's back at the hotel. She'd be able to tell us where to go." Sunny was still wiping the sleep from his eyes.

We found our girl behind her concierge desk. She was busy giving directions to a tourist. At the end of their conversation, she gave this older gent in a fedora a Waffle House coupon. I overheard the man ask if her if Waffle House really was the best place to find his medicine. "Ain't nothin Waffle House can't fix," she said.

The man in the fedora said, "You mean like a Po-boy?" I felt obliged to back her claims. "She's right. Sorry to be eavesdropping, but that restaurant works miracles."

"Feeling better?" Shaunice asked as the tourist left for Waffle House. "The older guy there, he said he was having issues with his back from driving all the way from California. He said he's on his way to Louisville."

"Kentucky? That's where we're headed!" Sunny said. "You know anything more about him?"

"No, not really. Said something about going to see a lawyer later tonight. Said something about horse racing, but he cut himself off right as you guys came up from behind."

"Anyway, Shaunice, we're new here. What's there to do on a Tuesday night?"

"You should go to Ponce City Market and walk around. After that, check out Edgewood. I know you guys like hip hop, so I figured you'd appreciate checking out Nayvadius DeMun Wilburn's roots."

"Who?"

"Future."

"The rapper?"

"Yes."

"Shaunice, you may just be the best ever concierge."

"Thanks," she said as she politely motioned for us to move aside. People were waiting behind us to ask her a question. In her hand, there were Waffle House coupons.

Sunny and I took an Uber over to Ponce City Market. After the Miracle At Waffle House, why consider doing anything other than what Shaunice advised? Although our trip's constitution called for relentless spontaneity, we felt like we couldn't go wrong following directives from our proven concierge. We were right about that in a big way which I'll now explain. There's a fine line to walk when travelling to parts unknown. How much of a trip unfolds as a result of reacting to your environment? How much of a trip is a result of careful, deliberate planning with no outside influence? Sunny and I were somewhere in between on that ancient continuum of how best to travel.

Ponce City Market is Atlanta's own version of Manhattan's Chelsea Market. Chelsea Market, located in the gentrified meatpacking district, used to be a Nabisco building. The Oreo cookie was invented in the Chelsea building long before developers in the '90s reimagined it into a shopping mall, food hall, and office building. The main access point to New York's High Line is next to Chelsea Market. The High Line is an elevated public walking corridor created on a former New York Central Railroad spur. In the northeast corner of Atlanta, an old Sears building along Ponce de Leon Avenue was redeveloped into Ponce City Market. There's even an adjacent elevated rail line that was converted to a public walkway. In Atlanta, it's called the BeltLine. The High Line was mimicked elsewhere in the US, including in Philly and Chicago.

Sunny and I didn't have any interest in shopping. We went straight to the BeltLine. The plan was to walk north the few miles to Piedmont Park and from there Uber our way down to Edgewood. On our walk, we discussed our options for the following day. It did not take us long to decide that we wanted to visit Memphis. To get there, we'd have to return through

Birmingham and then north and west up to southern Tennessee. There was lots to see and do in Memphis. Sun Records, Beale Street, Graceland, barbecue. After Memphis, who knows. Nashville? St. Louis was another option, although it was further out of the way.

It was about three quarters of the way toward Piedmont Park. The Belt-Line was busy that evening. People were out walking, jogging, hanging out. Sunny was going off on a tangent about cocktails in Memphis' ancient Peabody Hotel. One of Sunny's all time favourite movies is *The Firm* with Cruise and Hackman. Parts of that movie were shot at the Peabody, so I was getting an earful about all things *The Firm*.

"Sunny, I get it you want to go to the Peabody," I roared. Just as I said Sunny's name, I could've sworn I saw the old man from earlier at our hotel walk by.

"You see that?"

"What?"

"That guy from California, staying at our hotel, I think he just walked by?"

"Who?"

"The guy also going to Louisville. Could've sworn that was him just walked by."

"What was he wearing?"

"Well, it was different, but he still had that fedora on. That's why I'm not sure. But whoever that was, he winked at me. Do you remember what he was wearing in the lobby?"

"No idea. No way it was the same dude," Sunny said. "What're the odds?"

"I know, it's just...nevermind, you're probably right."

"You wanna turn around and see?"

"Nah. It's too busy, anyway. Let's just keep walking toward the park."

"You sure?"

"Yeah and I'm starving. Let's go to Edgewood, find us a bar to eat at."

"Yeah, I'm starving too."

"You just had a tray of food!"

"What're you talking about? I haven't had anything since those peanuts." Was I losing my mind? Was Sunny bullshitting?

Atlanta, off to a strange start.

It was dark when we got to Piedmont Park. Sunny hailed an Uber and in no time, we were let off on the corner of Edgewood Avenue and Randolph Street. Edgewood, we came to learn, is ground zero for a lot of influential hip hop culture that has permeated mainstream America. It's also a stone's throw from all things MLK. One block north was the birthplace of Martin Luther King Jr., his tombstone and the King Centre. The Ebenezer Baptist Church is next door to those institutions, MLK's former church. The bar we found was the only one with any activity. Later that night was Karaoke Night. There was a stage in the back, instruments included. As we sat and ate, more and more people started coming in from the chilly Atlanta night. An evening fog had settled in.

Sunny and I sat at the bar. Seated next to Sunny was a guy around our age. And further down were two drop dead beautiful girls. Sunny and I were the only white people in the place.

Sunny was asking the guy next to him about life in Atlanta. Russ was his name and he'd graduated from Georgia Tech five years ago. He was working in finance for Coca-Cola, which is headquartered in Atlanta. He said it was still a city young people like us could reasonably expect to buy a home in. Atlanta was good that way. Lots of culture, more affordable than San Francisco, New York, or Seattle. Leafy, hilly, Atlanta has four seasons, none of which are too extreme save for a few summer days. Traffic was a problem, but it was far better than LA. The airport could take you anywhere you want and jobs were plentiful. Russ was here to stay after moving to the city to attend college from his hometown of Indianapolis.

While I was listening, I couldn't keep my eyes off one of the girls seated at the end of the bar down from Russ. She was a goddess. Although I was on a break with my girlfriend, I still felt trepidation toward hitting on any woman. Sunny was also on a break and we agreed before we even got to New Orleans, a pact we made, that we would flirt only. The women we were on breaks with, we couldn't justify to ourselves anything more than that. So, I wanted to flirt with this bar queen. And seated next to her was her equally attractive friend. See where it went, what the hell. I went to the restroom first to make sure there wasn't any food in my teeth. I splashed some water on my face. There was something about that girl at the end of the bar.

When I came out of the restroom, she was still there. I was nervous. What would I say? She was probably there waiting for her boyfriend to show up. She was probably there to…I was talking myself out of it. What is it about our tendency to self sabotage? I could see in the corner of my eye a smile spread across Sunny's face. He knew what was going on as I walked past him.

"Hey."

Goddess: "Hi?"

"Tonight is karaoke night and I need a duet partner."

"Yeah?"

"Yeah. I thought you may be interested."

"What makes you say that?"

"I don't know. I just thought you might be interested." She looked at her friend. They both smiled like, is this guy for real?

"Honey, you know this ain't no country ass white bar."

"Do I look country?"

"You look like you just came from Disneyland. Who's your friend over there?

"Which one?"

"The only other white boy in this place."

"My cousin, Sunny."

"I like the look of him…" Her friend laughed. She was embarrassed.

"You want me to introduce you?"

"I don't know, sure…what you want to sing anyway? My friend Stacey's got an amazing voice. I don't sing at all."

"I'm Meko. Nice to meet you. I actually don't know what to sing, but I'm up for anything."

"You don't know what to sing? Even though you came over her seeing if we'd wanna join you?"

"Well, we can collaborate."

"Rhonda, you hear that? He don't even know what he wanna sing!"

"Meko? That's your name? You don't even know what you wanna sing? Are you for real?"

"Okay, ladies. How about if we are all still in this bar when the music starts, we can figure it out then. Sorry I asked!" I left in a huff back to my seat less than ten feet away.

Sunny: "What was that about?"

"Nevermind. Rhonda over there, she thinks you're cute."

Russ: "Those girls, they come here every karaoke night."

"Do they sing?" I asked.

"No."

"Lame."

"Stacey's boyfriend owns this place. He gets them to come in because, well, look at them… they attract people in. They are known around Edge-wood."

"What was that Russ?" Rhonda overheard. "You got something to say?"

"No ma'am, I was just was tellin' my new friends here that you guys are really talented singers when you want to be."

"I'll sing with your friend," Rhonda said of Sunny, the last guy to do karaoke.

"Sunny would love to," I said. "Wouldn't you."

"No, no, no. You're askin' the wrong guy."

Bartender: "Is there a problem here Stace?"

"These white boys wanna sing with us tonight."

"Yeah? Some George Strait?"

"BB King!" I shouted. "Singin' some BB King tonight."

Stacey: "BB King? You like BB King?"

"Love BB."

"What my dad listens to."

"Got good taste."

Bartender: "You actually wanna do BB King?"

"What I said wasn't it?"

"We got a bass and amp you want to plug-in? I got a guitar in the back."

"You play?"

"Yeah. Blues. This is a hip hop bar, but I dig the blues, man."

"Yeah me too. You wanna play some blues tonight? I'm Meko."

"Skip."

"Like James?"

"Yeah, like Skip James."

"Okay, all right." Rhonda was no longer talking. Stacey beamed in my direction.

"Tone's gonna like you," she said.

"You know, if I could sing pop tunes like Frank Sinatra or Sammy Davis Jr., I don't think I still could do it."

"Cause Lucille don't wanna play nothin' but the blues," Skip said, finishing my sentence.

"I think I'm pretty glad about that."

"I like the way Frank sings, the way Sammy sings, but I can get a little Frank, Sammy, a little Ray Charles, in fact, all the people with soul."

"A little Mahalia Jackson in there."

Skip got on his phone. "Tone, it's Skip. Got a white guy here says he can play the blues. You all right we play some blues tonight?" Skip nodded his head a few times. Wasn't saying anything, nodded his head a few more times. He closed his phone and looked in my direction.

"We got the go ahead. Why don't you plug in over there. You play bass? Play a couple tunes before I'm off. Tone's got someone gonna take my shift over. Let us play the blues."

"I knew Tone would dig," said Stacey. Rhonda was silent.

To the back of the building I went. That was where Skip had his instruments. There was a little stage back there too. I plugged in the bass, tuned it, started noodling around. It had been a while since I'd played.

Little while later, Sunny came back. "Meko, what the hell? You even know how to play?"

"You didn't know I played?"

"No! I did not know you played well enough to play in front of a crowd."

"Well, to be honest, I don't know either but hell, this is what this trip's about."

"Christ, you're gonna embarrass yourself. Then what?"

"Then we leave and we go back to Shaunice and tell her we had a great time and then get on the road and drive to Memphis. What's the big deal?"

"You see how many people are starting to show up?"

"No. I've been back here. Skip said he'd join in a minute."

"It's packed back there. Russ left, and now it's just me out there hangin' with Rhonda and Stacey."

"You guys gettin' along?"

"I'm gettin' shitfaced is what."

"Rhonda likes you. Hang in there. This'll be fun." Skip came back to join me. He was ready to play. He plugged in the little amps and tuned. He had an SG with him. He had a glass Coricidin bottle slide. This guy was a bluesman. "All right Meko, you ready? Wanna try a couple tunes 'fore we go out there? Christ it's busy out there. Tone did a social media blast. Said Future was here tonight."

"Shit, why'd he do that?"

"Tone does anything to get people in his bar. You sing?"

"Yeah, you're probably better."

"We'll trade back and forth."

"All right." Skip and I went out to the crowd and began our set. The crowd was chanting, "Future, Future, Future." When they saw us walk out, I heard a few people say: "The fuck?" First song, I was flubbing notes. Skip was perfect. His voice was gold. What was I getting myself into? "You get nervous, just play the root note, don't be all fancy, you hear?"

"Yeah. Okay. What key you like?"

"Let's go A to start. Follow my lead. All right, let's get this going." The karaoke sound guy configured our instruments and now we were connected to the entire bar's stereo system. Sunny told me later that from a block away, you could hear Skip's wailing guitar.

The doors to the bar were open and the inside of the place was packed. Skip led us off. We played a pop song to really get things going. Camila Cabello and Young Thug. It was a way to get the crowd into it. To my surprise, Stacey came up on stage and sang Camila's part while Skip rapped Thugger's part. I was just playin' the bass, trying not to look like an idiot. Stacey went back to the bar to sit with Rhonda. Rhonda by then had Sunny's full attention. They were laughing, talking. About what, I had the slightest clue.

"Okay now we gon' play a lil' blues for ya'll," I said to a crowd partially paying attention.

The crowd roared: "Where's Future!" The stage wasn't quite in the middle of the room. It was slightly off to the slide, which kept us from being the focal point. Again my attempt at playing bass wasn't going so well. I wasn't hitting the notes to BB King's *Lucille*. Skip looked over to me three quarters through the tune. He said, "You sure you know what you're doin'?"

"Yeah. Gotta I'll find the groove is all."

"All right, all right. We can't do many more of that. This crowd will leave, Tony will freak and I'll be out a job."

"Really?"

"Let's just play it right, okay?" Meanwhile, I'm thinking, damn, I need me some Waffle House to help me get along. Waffle House! That was it. In between our next song, I called out to Sunny and he came up to where I was playing. Sunny, drunkern hell now. "Sunny, I need you to get me some Waffle House, help me get along here."

"You need what?"

"Waffle House! Get Rhonda to take you to the nearest one, get me a pecan waffle to go. If it helped you, it'll help me."

Sunny went with Rhonda to get me some Waffle House. Half an hour later, Sunny showed up with a to-go bag. Meanwhile, Skip and I had been labouring through. Well, I was. He was holding it all together. Though by that time, a buddy of his joined on drums. And he and Stacey were trading lead vocals. When Skip was singing, Stacey would sing harmony. They were terrific. So good that despite my inability to play the way I knew, more and more people showed up. A blues show on Edgewood Ave wasn't something they heard too often. The cries for Future were abating. Tony was behind the bar counting the bills. In between the second and third set of our show, I scarfed down the Waffle House. The effect was immediate. We came back to the stage and I was finally *playing*. Skip looked over, thinking, who the hell just showed up? Stacey thinking the same.

Skip was playing his own tunes. And he was talking to the crowd in between songs like a pro. He was talking his lyrics too. We got into some jump blues. *Bloodshot Eyes*, Wynonie Harris. To do it the way he was doing it takes the kind of subtle rhythm you're born with. "I used to sing spirituals and I thought that this was the thing that I wanted to do," he said before one of our songs. "But somehow or other when I went in the army..." at the mention of the army, there were a few boos, a few cheers. "Well, now I'm paying my dues. Maybe you don't know what I mean when I say paying dues. I mean when things are bad with me, I can always, I can always, you know like depend here on my blues." Skip starts wailing on his SG, I'm in a Waffle House trance and Stacey's looking over from her side of the stage like what kind of night is this?

After our show, the crowd didn't die down. We were the talk of Edgewood. Skip and I and Stacey and our drummer Kayvon. I don't think Tony's bar will ever get that busy again. He was over capacity on a Tuesday night.

But what happened next was horrible. The guys in the bar started brawling. The root of the brawl was Sunny. See, Rhonda's ex-boyfriend showed up. Just out of prison and on parole, first thing he saw was a hand on Rhonda's inner thigh. That hand belonged to Sunny who was also whispering in her ear. They were seated in the corner, oblivious to the world around them. The guy came up to Rhonda and grabbed her by the arm and dragged her off the couch. Now, Sunny gets mad. And when Sunny gets angry, watch out.

Sunny and the guy start swingin' fists and then Rhonda gets in between them. She gets pushed over accidentally and she falls on an old gas tank burning for heat. Tony had set these things up around the place to give his establishment the hip vintage look. Gas ran all over the floor and the building, it caught on fire. We almost didn't make it out of there. From the street, we watched as Tony's place went up in flames. Thankfully, everyone made it out okay. The crowd, Stacey, Rhonda, Sunny, myself, Tony. Rhonda's ex-boyfriend fled the scene with tears streaming down his face. It was an insane end to the night. The fire trucks came, but it was too late. As we watched the building burn, Skip said he would rename his guitar Rhonda after the brawl and fire she started.

It was the middle of the night when we got back to our hotel. The Waffle House was still open and so that's where we went for a little late night chow. The only other people in the restaurant at that ungodly hour was an eastern European construction crew on their way to work. A new high rise going up nearby and these were the guys doing the work. Sunny and I stood behind the pack of guys. We couldn't understand a word they were saying. The people we'd seen earlier in the day working weren't there anymore. It was a new crew and they were extremely slow. Sunny was grow-ing impatient. He was also sobering up and there would most certainly be a hangover to contend with.

Waffle House was there for us to get Sunny through his salt episode. Waffle House was there to get me my groove back on stage. Would Waffle House be there to help Sunny along with his impending doom? The con-struction crew eventually cleared out of the way and we ordered waffles and toast and hash browns. Sunny suggested we order coffee and just get on the road to Memphis. I vetoed that. We needed rest. Sunny and I grabbed a booth near the corner window.

Now that was a good meal at that hour in Atlanta. Waffle House, three for three. I had eaten a pecan waffle only a few hours earlier. And with each bite, the complexion on my eating partner's face improved. Miracle food. From where I was seated, the pack of construction guys sat directly in my view. They were working insane hours, yet they were quite happy to joke among themselves, throwing French Fries at one another. I recall being in similar late night restaurants and food fights erupting between strangers. That night, there were no food fights, only fists at Tony's.

Sunny and I didn't discuss the brawl at Tony's. It wasn't because it wasn't on our minds. It was the sight of the old man in the fedora that diverted my attention. Sitting at the opposite side of the restaurant, there he was. The construction guys had left. Up to then, they had blocked him from my sight. He was facing away from us. I'd had enough of this guy. It was not a mere coincidence that we saw him now three times in one day. What was he doing at this hour, at his age? Didn't add up.

"Sunny, see that guy back there?" Sunny looked up at me with a mouth full of waffle, turns around to see.

"Yeah, what about him?"

"Same guy, I think."

"Which one? From Tony's?"

"No. From earlier. Remember when we were on the BeltLine and I..."

"That's him?"

"Think it is."

"What's he doing here?"

"He's been following us."

"You serious?"

"I'm gonna go find out."

"You're what?"

"I'm gonna go talk to the guy. Stay here, keep an eye, okay? Something goes wrong...well, you know."

Across the Waffle House I walked. He was carefully eating his plate of eggs, reading a day old copy of the Atlanta Journal-Constitution. I cleared my throat. "Excuse me." He either didn't hear or was ignoring me. Cleared my throat again. "Excuse me." This time louder. Still nothing. "Hey pal! Who you think?"

"Sit down," he said, quiet and polite.

"Excuse me?"

"Sit down. Please." He continued to read his paper. He was perfectly calm and intent on finishing the story. He took another sip of coffee, put the paper back together, folded it up and looked me in the eye. His stare was perfectly calm. His face was clean. There was age around his piercing blue eyes. The dark fedora was perfectly kept and square on his head. He stared right at me.

"I keep seeing you."

"To get your attention, yes."

"About what?"

"Saturday."

"The Derby?"

"My partner and I, we're looking for some help. Are you and Sunny interested?"

"How do you know his name? You know mine?"

"Of course, Meko. My business partner and I are looking for help. Are you interested?"

"Come again? Who you are?" The old man stared. Perfectly calm.

"My business partner and I need help. Are you and..."

"Sunny interested. Yeah, I hear you. Sure. You need a tire changed?"

"Are you interested in helping?"

"All right, listen pal, I'm outta here..." I stood up to leave. As I turned around, the old man asked again for me to sit down.

"Sit down, Meko. We can help you with Von Rotz." Mention of Von Rotz's name had me seated without hesitation. "But, you want our help, we'll need your help."

"How do you know Von Rotz?"

"My business partner and I are looking for help. Are you and Sunny interested?"

"Okay, fine, yes, sure. Sunny and I are interested in helping you and your business partner."

"Good," he said, blinking for the first time. It was as if a pebble had been tossed into a perfectly calm lake that was the old man's general demeanour.

"I am headed to Louisville, and we've come to believe you and Sunny are too. Correct me if I am wrong."

"That's right," I said.

"And you hope to win money?"

"Yes...among other things."

"Like?"

"Well, we are going to have some fun too."

"Well, of course. But you are going because you hope to win money to help your friend out with his medical bills, am I right?"

"Bingo. Do I even dare ask how you know any of this? What's your name anyway?"

"Decker."

"Decker?"

"Sam Decker." He slid his card toward me. I took it, saving to look at it for later.

"Okay Sam Decker, how the hell you know so much about Sunny and me anyway?"

"Now's not the time for that. All I need to know is whether you and your cousin Sunny are interested in helping..."

"You and your business partner. Yeah, I got it, and like I said, sure pal. To be honest, Sam Decker, or whatever your name is, I don't quite know if it's us you want to help you."

"Oh, no, we're quite certain we would like your help. Quite certain. Meko, take this." He slid an envelope across the table. "Wait until you're back in your room to look at what's inside. I'll be seeing you soon." Decker got up. He put his coat on and slid a one hundred dollar bill underneath the bill for his breakfast. "Good to see you, Meko. My business partner and

I, we're thrilled you and Sunny are on board." After Decker left, I looked at his card. It was basic black and white. Sam Decker in bold letters. Beneath his name, *Principal*. On the other side was a silhouetted thoroughbred in full stride. Underneath the image of the horse, it read *Tassajara Racing*.

Sunny said, "He knew our names? He knew Von Rotz? What?" We were packing our things up later that morning after only a few hours sleep. It wasn't yet ten in the morning. We had to get on the road. Sunny asked me who Sam Decker was after seeing the business card on the bedside table. "I'll tell you in the car. We gotta go if we want to get to Memphis in good time. And there's another stop I think we should make on our way. I'll explain. Come on, Sunny, let's go."

In the hotel lobby on our way out, I saw Shaunice standing behind the concierge desk. She was smiling as we approached. She said she heard about the fire last night. "And I trust you convened with Mr. Decker?"

"You know that guy? Who is he? Meko won't tell me till we're in the car."

"What do you mean? He said you were close friends?"

"When did you first talk to him?"

"He called before ya'll even got here, can't remember exactly what, but he said ya'll be travelling in a group together or something."

"News to me. Anyway, thanks Shaunice, and thanks for the Waffle House and Edgewood recommendations. Gotta say, Atlanta has not been without its fair share of surprises."

"Enjoy the rest of your trip."

Sunny didn't believe it. He didn't think that some stranger named Sam Decker not only knew our names, where we were headed and for what reason. He also didn't believe it when I showed him the envelope Decker had given me. In the envelope, there was a piece of paper. Typewritten on that piece of paper was the word Shey Gompa. Below Shey Gompa, there was an address: 917 Old Taylor Road, Oxford, Mississippi. Below the address, there was a time and date: May 2, 2018. 3 p.m.

Atlanta sure was a trip. Shaunice, Waffle House, Edgewood, Decker, all of these experiences added to something that looks preposterous in hindsight. But then, is this not what travel is all about? Sunny and I discussed some but not all of what happened. Mainly, we focused on Von Rotz and what his interpretation of our previous twenty-four hours would look like. Sunny thought that it was Von Rotz that put Decker onto us. It wasn't a bad theory. I wasn't ready to come to any conclusions. We just assumed that whatever was waiting for us in Oxford would help explain our trip's increasingly foggy landscape through the Dear Old Southland.

We didn't have time to stop at Talladega if we wanted to make it to Oxford by three in the afternoon. But we did have time to do a quick driving tour of Atlanta's downtown. We saw the CNN building, we drove along Ted Turner Drive, drove past the gargantuan Mercedes-Benz football stadium, and then we were back on I-20 bound for Birmingham. We had something like five hours of driving ahead of us before Oxford and then from Oxford, it was about an hour north to Memphis.

In the car, Sunny read more about betting. Like what superfecta meant. To place a superfecta bet, you put money on the horses that come in first, second, third and fourth place — in that exact order. The previous year, a superfecta paid out $75,000 on a one dollar bet. We salivated over that number. Sunny also found out that a horse named Justify was the one everyone expected to win this year. If we put Justify in our one slot, which horses would fill the remaining three? Justify had 5-2 odds. Next came Mendelssohn and My Boy Jack, both with 6-1 odds. Audible was the four horse at 7-1. Although Justify was the favourite, by no means did that mean the outcome was certain. That's horse racing. We weren't oblivious to that. We also weren't oblivious to the fact that the oddsmakers can be very wrong.

Sunny: "And all he said was, I'll be seeing you soon?"

"That's what he said."

"Well...shit! Wait, what?" Sunny was in disbelief. As was I, but at least I had the benefit of actually meeting the guy.

"You realize that's today, right?"

"You saying we should go to Oxford?"

"We have the time and it is on our way to Memphis..."

"What's waiting for us there?"

"No clue. Do you know what Shey Gompa means?"

"No, what?"

"I looked it up. Buddhist temple, eastern Himalaya."

"Huh?"

"What I can't seem to understand is how we can be of help to Decker," I said settling into the freeway.

"What do you mean?"

"Well, he kept asking me if you and I were interested in helping him and his business partner out. That was the key question that I had to answer before he gave me the envelope."

"Where was I when all this happened again?"

"Asleep on a pile of waffles."

"Right."

"Anyway, I get the feeling that whatever we find at that address in Oxford, it will have something to do with us helping Decker out. I don't know. I mean, look, what's the sense of agonizing over this. We already have a betting strategy that we know probably won't payout. But that's life and we are okay with it. We have our hopes, but we can't reasonably expect to actually win the kind of money to help out Von Rotz."

"What if what we find in Oxford gets us that much closer to getting the money?"

"I'm not sure. I mean, what if we get roped into something against the law? You think the Derby is rigged? You think we may have the keys to the kingdom?"

"Keys to what kingdom?"

"Do you think maybe this Decker guy knows how the horses will finish?"

"Christ, I don't know. Why don't you ask him next time he pays us a visit?"

"Yeah but he didn't say how or when or where."

"This is weird."

"Hell yeah it is. But what can we do about it?"

"Well, we could just skip going to Oxford, go straight to Memphis and pretend this crazy Atlanta episode never even happened."

"True, we could..."

"But we're not gonna."

"We can't."

"Because going to Oxford, that's..."

"...What Von Rotz would do."

"And we're on this trip for no other reason, right?"

"Right."

"So..."

"We're going to Oxford." We said it at the same time.

What was in Oxford, anyway? We had no idea. As I drove, Sunny looked the place up. Oxford is steeped in all kinds of fascinating history. It's a college town, like Tuscaloosa. Ole Miss is a stone's throw from the little downtown area. Other facts: there's an impressive literary culture there. Faulkner lived and worked there. Grisham lives and works there. And in between those heavyweights, all kinds of writers that no one will ever know existed in a place called Oxford, Mississippi. Their work is maybe found in at local library, at a local independent book store. For every Faulkner, for every Grisham, there are hundreds, thousands, who also wrote down their thoughts, told a story on a page. Most have been forgotten through the merciless sands of time. Is a remembered author, a known author, nothing more than the result of good marketing? Writers submit their stories to a business that's called a publisher. That business does its business by selling pages bound between a cover. John Grisham's publisher has sold three hundred million odd books with the Grisham name. John Grisham didn't do the selling. He only wrote the story down.

Sunny and I talked about this as we drove. Sunny, far more interested in the business world, explained to me his thoughts on why it's not content that's king. "Content is king" is a maxim believed by many. To say content is king is to be conventional. Sunny's take is distribution is king. We were listening to his Spotify. The new Drake record had just dropped and it was all that anyone was talking about. And Drake had Big Freedia on his biggest track. We had just seen crazy Big Freedia perform at Jazz Fest. A wild, absurdist show. The musicians we hear on Spotify, the ones we love, are, for the most part, thanks to distribution. Canned music. Records. You can write and play music that makes the Beatles, Beethoven sound like amateurs. But the masses will never know without that music being shown to them. To Sunny, distribution is king. If a composer wrote the most beautiful symphony the world has ever seen, how will anyone know without first hearing it?

* * *

Lula Mae, I know what you're thinking. You think the Atlanta segment of Run For Roses is complete fiction. You're probably thinking either it's Meko spinning one hell of a tall tale, or it's me, the story's relayer, making all this up. As God as my witness, I promise you that I am doing my very best to record down to you in these letters precisely what I am being told. Whether you believe the story or not, entirely up to you.

I will say that Meko, not once while telling his story, mixed up his details. Not once has he course corrected. Not once has he...you get the point. It's been a consistent narrative the entire time we've been in the car. Sure, there have been breaks between him continuing the story, but that has more to do with us reacting to the road trip we are on. Am I able to say that Meko and I have had any experiences even remotely close to what you've just read? No. What happened in Atlanta, truth be told, I have a hard time believing it too. I mean, ain't nothin' Waffle House can't fix...can that actually be true? And, I've never heard Meko play the bass. But I do know he's played music before. As for Decker, that was the first time I've ever heard his name.

Though I must say, given the fact that we are going on this road trip only several months after Meko and Sunny did their Run For Roses, I can't help but think maybe there's a connection to Decker and why we are on our way to San Francisco. Tassajara was the giveaway. It's a name that has a ring to it. I had to look that name up. And if you do look up Tassajara, the first thing you'll find is the Tassajara Hot Springs east of Carmel, California. There's nothing more about the place I know of. I have no clue if there's any connection between the hot springs, horse racing, Sam Decker, or anything. What I will say is if we find ourselves driving south toward Monterey after we get to San Francisco, my ears will most certainly perk. But I can't get ahead of myself. Who knows, maybe Meko and Sunny never even got to Oxford. I don't even know if Von Rotz is still alive! There's no use in jumping ahead. All I can do is be the best I can be at listening to this strange tale unfold.

Anyway, it's almost two in the morning and I am exhausted after writing this all out. Please forgive me for my substandard prose. I've never done anything like this before. Still no sign of Meko. Should I be worried? I don't know. He's reliable. He's been around. This road trip ain't his first.

He said he was going to listen to some live music. Okay, I am going to stop worrying. I am looking forward to tomorrow. We are supposed to be going as far south as Fort Bragg, just north of the idyllic coastal town Mendocino. Be well, speak soon, hugs and kisses!

NOVEMBER 5

Dear Lula Mae,

I write this to you not from a motel, but a hotel. Yes, today is the first time thus far in our trip south that Meko has splurged. Tonight, we are staying at the Mendocino Hotel. It's old, it's wooden, the exterior is painted a fresh canary yellow. A guy is playing old ragtime piano down-stairs. I'm expecting Mark Twain himself to come waltzing in from a Sierra Nevada mining claim. Don't get me wrong, I'll be the first to proclaim my love for the ground floor, roadside motel. But to stay at a place like this one? I wish you could be here to see it. Today was one of the better days of travel. Not many hours in the car and lots of time spent among the giant Redwoods. Humboldt Redwoods State Park is a place I really think you should visit one day.

The redwoods are plentiful and large in that part of California. Of course, together, the Redwoods make forests. These forests are deep with shades of rust reds, blues and ambers. To walk through these forests, or run as we did, is to feel as if you are truly a part of nature. It's hard to articulate what I mean. Among the Redwoods, the air is thicker, sweeter, restorative. It must be enriched with oxygen. The light that makes it through the dense upper canopy of these forests makes you think you are in a kingdom of gi-ant trees that belongs on another world. It sounds far fetched for me to say it like that, but these forests are just so different from any other forest I've ever seen.

And then, after a while, you notice the trees individually. Now your sen-sory system is free to tune in to the particulars of that giant tree that is right

in front of you. That tree is so large in both vertical and horizontal directions that you can't help but stop for further inspection. The bark is wonderfully ruddy. The moss grows in freedom across the tree trunk and over
the many limbs. The life that uses each tree for their home: The bugs, the
birds, the snakes, the snails, the fungi, the microbes, it's all there. And so
long as you mind their business, these life forms will gladly accept you into
their warm hearth. Although in these deep forests, it may at first feel cooler
than if standing on the outer edge underneath direct sunlight, spend
enough time in a grove of Redwoods and that coolness will be replaced by a
new kind of warmth. You don't disagree with this unique warmth. You
bask in it, you run it, you jump in it. If you have more time than Meko and
me, you live in this warmth. To spend a few weeks camping in the Redwoods is to give your soul a chance to sit down beside a warm fire burning
in the dead cold of a winter's night.

My theory is that our sun's warmth moves in a more complex fashion
underneath the canopy of a a grove of Redwoods. The trees take in the sun,
and the trees distribute among their friends the sun's harnessed power. The
trees work together. One corner of a forest may be in deficit of energy from
the sun, and sensing this, from across the forest, another group of trees
gladly exchanges surplus energy to their friends. The trees work together.
They are in concert with one another and the soil that hosts their roots and
the air that suspends their branches and leaves. These forests are singular
organizations. Each Redwood forest and there aren't many of them, are
made up of individual trees. But the forest's strength isn't a result of adding
up the strength of each individual tree. No, the strength of a forest is accre-
tive. The sum is greater than the parts. It's a miracle of nature.

These thoughts I have of the California Redwoods, perhaps you can tell
that Meko and I have been exploring the words of the early pioneers. There
is the standard bible found on the bedside table in this hotel room, but
there are also the journals of the people who chose to live here in the nine-

teenth century. Contemporaries of people like John Muir. It's lovely stuff
to read. The way they frame the meaning of what a forest can be.

A lot of their theories, at least the ones I am reading in these journals, I
think would've been cutting edge back then. Today's modern science can
explain much of what these people were trying to articulate, but isn't it interesting to hear of forests as the kind of organization that I just referred
to? The exchange of surplus energy, yadda yadda. That came from a journal dated 1844 by J.P. Donnelly. There is no more information about who
J.P. was and why he was in California at that time.

Maybe they were onto something. The forward of this book that I am
reading was written by a Stanford ecology Ph.D. twenty years ago. He
points out that many of the concepts and themes and questions that the
early naturalists considered are much the same as the concepts and themes
and questions considered today. The difference is the language used, word
choice. To that end, I suppose it's true that what Socrates was contemplat-
ing is no different than what you and I contemplate. Of course, once you
distill it all down to the true essence. Anyway, I am rambling now. But I
can't help it. There's something about the northern California coastline
and the inland forests. It's a magical place. At least for me, it inspires me to
give myself permission to explore uncommon topics and questions. And I
don't mean to say that the lands we've travelled across to get here are any
less awe-inspiring. As I've said in previous letters, the rugged, raw beauty of
the Oregon coastline is in a category of its own.

Maybe it just took this long for my senses to open up to the natural environment around me. Maybe it took this long to shake the artificiality of
urban, concrete Seattle? But I like Seattle. I'm tempted to say this is conun-
drum territory, that of balancing the natural and the urbane, but I will stop
myself there. Life is about balance. It takes living through a cold, hard winter to appreciate the warmth of a warm night in July. It takes the bitterness
of a cup of coffee to appreciate the sweetness of chocolate. You appreciate

the glass of water more when you are thirsty. When is there a point in our lives when we are not reacting to a prior state? Even when we decide to be proactive, does that not come about from feeling like we've been living too...reactive?

Life is about balance, I am convinced. Do we ever achieve lasting balance? Maybe, maybe not. I think we are continually oscillating between states of deficit and surplus. Deficit and surplus in the realms of both the emotional and the physical. It's all connected. Now, that's not to say that I don't think that we can achieve balance, harmony. I think we can. When we do, it's a wonderful feeling. It's a feeling of deep relief. But it doesn't last forever. Nor should it. Again, here I am rambling. Blame the Redwoods.

Today I was awe-inspired. But there was also a low point. It had to do with money. First, I should point out that the only time we got off the 101, despite being miles and miles from the coast, was to take a slight detour along the Avenue of the Giants. There is a stretch of California coastline that has no substantial highway running alongside. You have no choice but to drive inland. On this drive inland is when you navigate through the Redwoods. Next to the 101, for a brief stretch, there is the Avenue of the Giants, near the town of Myers Flat (population, 146). Near Myers Flat, there are several colossal trees that somehow have fallen under private ownership. Not the state, but private individuals. These individuals charge a fee to see "their" tree. Not only do they charge a fee, but they've decorated the land around the tree to puff up the allure of the place to the air-conditioned tourist. It's nothing more than greedy commercialism, you ask me. These trees should not be dressed up, marketed, signed, and gift shopped. To do so, to think this is a justifiable means to earn a living, it's missing the point entirely. When we saw what was going on in that part of the Avenue of the Giants, Meko and I got out of there real quick. Makes me sick. Anyway, I won't use up any more ink on this topic. But let it be known: crass commercialism is a disease found even in the depths of California's Redwood forests.

You're probably thinking, okay here we go, buddy spends a few hours in a forest and he comes out the other side a wide-eyed, tree huggin', kumbayá singin' hippie. Share the land, capitalism is evil, and on and on. I just mean that if you were to see the operation those people have set up, selling access to these ancient trees, I know you'd agree with what I am saying. There are other ways to make a buck in this world.

After driving inland, eventually you come to a fork in the road at the town of Leggett. Travelling north to south, a left turn keeps you on the 101. The 101 stays inland and will eventually take you through Santa Rosa and finally over the Golden Gate Bridge into downtown San Francisco. A right turn puts you on Highway 1. Along this road, you drive along California's coastline until you have to merge back onto the 101 to cross over the bridge. So, it was along Highway 1 that we first came to Fort Bragg and then a little further south, Mendocino.

A few blocks from our hotel, a little grocer sells fresh produce and deli sandwiches. As the sun fell, Meko and I ate our dinner of fruits and sandwiches and vegetables on a picnic table. We ate strawberries, artichoke sandwiches and spinach salad. The sun was warm on our faces, but the evening air turned cool once it was gone. A November night on California's northern coastline does not stay as warm as you may think. Next, the stars came out. Shards of light from the interior of the grocer splashed onto our table as we ate. We were in no rush. When we got back to the hotel, Meko stayed downstairs at the bar. He wanted to hear more ragtime piano. He wanted to talk to the pretty waitress. I left him there and walked up the old wooden staircase to the room we shared. From this room, I write you this letter. And for the rest of this letter, my aim is to tell you what happened between Atlanta and Memphis, Tennessee.

Sincerely,
Foxworth

* * *

How Sunny and Meko discovered William Faulkner's old house; How Meko learned the hard way how to eat Memphis barbecue and how Meko received unexpected help at the Peabody Hotel from the cabalistic Snakeskin.

We hauled ass to get from Atlanta to Oxford before three in the afternoon. We stopped only once on the outskirts of Birmingham for gas. Aside from that one stop, it was a direct shot all the way. I drove, going ninety miles an hour for most of it. We got to Oxford with fifteen minutes to spare. We both were hungry. We would have to wait until after our visit to 916 Old Taylor Road.

To get to 916, you drive south from the heart of town on South Lamar Boulevard. After a couple miles, you turn right onto Old Taylor and travel half a mile to a bend in the road. At the bend, there is a long cedar lined driveway to a beautiful, old Greek revival designed house situated among thick north Mississippi forest. The house had a name: Rowan Oak. The house had a history. One of its former occupants could sure write. His name was William Faulkner.

Rowan Oak is now a museum. There's a curator and if you want a tour, you need to make an appointment. The place has regular business hours. So why, at three in the afternoon on Wednesday, May 2, was Rowan Oak's entrance gate closed and locked? No matter, Sunny and I got out of our rented Focus and hopped the gate. Down the tree lined path we walked. There was a wind. The sky above was charcoal. Soon, it would rain. There was nobody around. It was a dead quiet afternoon save for the tree leaves rustling in the sporadic wind. What is it about Mississippi and these ghostly antebellum atmospheres? Where were Chauncey and Longstreet?

The pathway leading to the house is out of a dream. It's manicured, well kept. There was a wide contrast between the serene landscape surrounding

Sunny and me and our nerves. Well, my nerves, at least. I don't know what Sunny was thinking. He'd never met Decker, and his run in with Chauncey didn't seem to phase him one bit. Whereas the experience I had in Longstreet's house, and the perplexing meeting with Decker, both had me on edge. Sunny led the way. I think he just wanted to get whatever was going to happen over with and find a place to eat and talk to some Ole Miss sorority girls. I often envy Sunny's temperament.

Sunny said, "What you wanna do for food after this? Eat here or haul ass up to Memphis?"

"How about both?"

"I was hoping you'd say that. So, what are we expecting to happen here?"

"I don't know. All I have to go by is the note Decker gave me." I handed Sunny the envelope. He opened it and took out the sparsely typewritten note.

"This is so weird."

"I know. But hell, maybe we'll get a tip on how to bet at the Derby."

"Didn't we already decide that my approach was the way we'd go?"

"Well, yeah, but I mean, that was before we encountered this Decker guy."

"And what makes you think he can help us again?"

"It's more a hunch. Course, had you not been passed out on a plate of waffles and sitting next to me, you'd probably be thinking along the same lines as me."

"That or I'da thought this whole thing was insane."

"True, but either way, we didn't have any plans to check out Faulkner's old house."

"Remind me who Faulkner is again?"

"Really?"

"Yeah, really. Not everyone reads books written by dead people."

Just as I was about to tell Sunny who William Faulkner was, the front door of Rowan Oak slowly opened. We were about fifty yards away. We couldn't see if anyone was in the doorway. There were no lights on inside the house. Was it the wind that opened the door?

Sunny: "You think the wind opened the door?"

"That's a heavy door. No way."

"But no one's there!"

"That we can see. Sunny Shhh. Let's keep quiet."

"Screw that. HEY!" Sunny yelled. "WHO'S THERE?"

"Sunny, shut up!"

"No, Meko. This is ridiculous. HEY! ANYONE THERE?"

Nothing. From the east, a strong gust of wind blew the door wide open and there we were standing on Rowan Oak's front step with a clear view into the 19th-century mansion.

"Christ, what's going on here?" Sunny said.

He looked at his watch. It was three on the nose. We stopped for a moment. There was the sound of wind, nothing more. The house was empty. It was dark. Drops of rain began falling from the sky. Through the door, I walked. Sunny followed at first and then stopped.

"I think I'll walk around the house while you go in. Sound good?"

"Hell no! Stay with me. Come on. Let's go."

"Okay, fine."

There was an entryway staircase before us as we walked in. Inside, the house was no warmer than the cool, stormy outside temperature. I went up the stairs. Sunny stayed on the main floor. Upstairs, there were a few different rooms connected by a hallway. A door led out to the upstairs front porch, directly overhead the house's main entrance. The door was locked. I unlocked it and walked onto the balcony. Now, it was raining. The winds were still up. I stood there, thinking things over, trying to remember the nature of my conversation with Decker. Nothing about it stood out. What was supposed to happen at Rowan Oak at three in the afternoon?

"Hey Sunny," I called, returning into the house, locking the door behind me.

"Yeah?"

"You think he meant three in the morning?"

Sunny said nothing.

"Sunny?" Nothing.

"Sunny, where are ya? I called again as I returned to the main floor.

"Over here. Meko, come take a look at what I just found."

I found Sunny bent over the kitchen table. He was flipping his way through a big coffee table book.

"What is it?"

"It's one of those books where people sign their name, where they're from. Look at this, your pal Decker's on here."

"Decker? Sam Decker?"

"If Samuel Decker is the same dude you ran into at the Waffle House then yeah."

"Let me see that." I grabbed the book from the table. Sure enough, there was the name Samuel Decker written in cursive handwriting. The time and date signed: Quarter to three, Wednesday, May 2. I looked at Sunny who said: "That mean he's here?" We looked around. Still, there was nothing. Far as we could tell, we were the only people in that crazy old house. Sunny signed our names before we went back outside.

"Wanna walk around the back?"

"Sure," Sunny said. "But let's make it quick, we're gonna get sick, we stay out here too long."

"Come on, let's check it out and then we'll go back to town for soup or something. Warm up."

There was a large yard behind the house fenced with horizontal two by fours spaced apart. In the far corner of the yard, there was a small, derelict barn. The barn's state of disrepair was odd, given the immaculate condition of the main house. The door to the barn was locked and there were no windows to look through.

"Come on, Meko, let's get out of here. I'm getting soaked."

"One sec," I said as I walked to the barn's rear.

"Sunny, take a look at this. There's a pathway behind here leading out to the woods."

"I'm sure there is. But at this point, I don't care. Come on, let's go. I have no idea what the hell we're doing here."

"You want, just go back to the car. I'm gonna go take a look and see what's back there."

"Meko, we're getting soaked, man! Let's just go and eat and drive up to Memphis. We'll get to the Peabody in time for cocktail hour."

I wouldn't listen. So, Sunny returned to the Focus to wait. "Fifteen minutes, okay? You're not back at the car in fifteen, I am outta here and I am not gonna come look for your sorry ass in those damn woods."

The wind was howling as I made my way into those damn woods. I can't recall how I was feeling at the time. I remember thinking this whole scenario was just one more extension of an increasingly supernatural road trip. Come to think of it, I was feeling pretty good. I had an enormous amount of adrenaline running through me, and I don't even think I noticed how dour the weather had turned. I didn't even notice, not until I met up with Sunny again, how wet and soggy and muddy I got.

What I did notice, in those woods behind Rowan Oak, was nothing really out of the ordinary. Nothing that you wouldn't expect. As I gingerly walked my way through the dark, wet forest, all that I could hear was my own breath, the sound of the wind and rain, and the many twigs and branches crunching beneath my shoes. The wind whistled. My senses, hyper-tuned to my surrounding environment. A fierce gust came, and the whistle, for a brief moment, I could've sworn it sounded like the whistle of a young woman. I stopped walking. Another gust came and again, there was that whistle. It was clearly a whistle from a human. It had to be. No way could that sound originate from an inanimate object. Fear gripped me. Who else was in these woods? "Hello? Who's there?" I called. "Anyone? Sunny? That you whistling?" Nothing.

Slowly, carefully, I looked around. I could see nothing except for dense forest. I continued walking on the path that grew narrower by the yard. A few minutes passed without another whistle. I picked up my pace. Up ahead and to the right, I could see the outline of...a building? A pump house? I couldn't tell. The rain and the trees obfuscated my field of view. If what I was now walking on could still be called a path, to get to the distant pump house, structure, whatever it was, I had to traipse my way through thick brush and off what little remained of the path leading back to Rowan Oak.

I was right. It was an old pump house. It was a small one, the size of an outhouse. It had been years, probably decades since anyone had used it. There was a door kept closed by a wooden handle. Inside, there were cob-webs, moss, and nothing much else. As I closed the door, there was that whistle again. It was startlingly loud. I whirled around. I was breathing heavy now. "Who's there?" Nothing.

From where I now stood, I couldn't see anything except the surround-ing forest. Had I not just come from a stately old mansion, I never would've guessed that a few hundred yards away, there was exactly that. Had there not been the pump house to anchor the direction in which I'd just travelled, how easy to get lost. I jogged back through the dense woods to the path. From the path, I ran back to the barn. Never again did I hear the whistle despite the winds and rain. I ran back around the house to the front. I didn't bother stopping except for the last moment before the house fell from view along the winding driveway.

Catching my breath, I turned around for one last look. Nothing was different about the place. That was my initial impression. But then I saw it. The Edison bulb hung above the front porch entranceway. It was on! Who turned it on? Sunny must've been able to see me where I was standing. He honked the horn a couple times. I looked to see if I could see him. I wanted to show him the light. I couldn't see the car, however. I turned around again for one more look at the shining light. It was shining no more. Whoever had turned the light on, it was now off.

I ran back to the car. Sunny was inside listening to Fred McDowell. The door was locked and I banged on the passenger side window. Startled, he looked up and saw a dark figure outside the car. He couldn't tell if it was me.

"Sunny, open the damn door!" He opened the door and I jumped in. My face, my hair, my clothes, everything was soaked.

"Meko, what the hell happened?"

"Let's just get outta here, okay? Hurry, drive, come on." Sunny put the car in gear and back to town we drove.

Our waitress asked for our orders. I was in shock from what did and didn't happen at Rowan Oak. Sunny was on carefree highway, jonesing to get to the Peabody. We didn't have much time. I asked for whatever the cafe was known for. Situated in the heart of town, we found this little place next to an ancient bookstore with, of course, its fair share of Faulkner. The waitress suggested we try their fried okra. Sunny and I both went for it and a cup of coffee.

"How come ya'll're so wet?" The waitress said, pouring coffee.

"Went out to Faulkner's old house, got soaked checking out the woods behind the house."

"You went to Bailey Woods?"

"That's what they're called?"

"Bailey Woods, yeah. They had it open?"

"Well, no. To be honest, we jumped the gate."

"Figured you musta."

"Why's it closed anyway?"

"Kids been vandalizin' the place for the past couple weeks now. Curator had to do something. You go and see Faulkner's grave? The headstone been all smashed up too jus' the other day."

Sunny: "Meko didn't tell you why we went there though. When we were in Atlanta yesterday, some guy told us to be at 917 Old Taylor Road at three in the afternoon. So we haul ass all the way from Atlanta to make it in time and there's nothing to be found."

"Why would you even want to in the first place? Drive all the way from Atlanta. Lord thas a long way."

"Well we thought he would give us some sort of idea as to how to bet at the Derby, which is where we plan to be on Saturday. See, a close friend of ours is really sick and we want to try and win money at the Derby to help with his medical bills."

"And to buy back his sailboat," I added.

Waitress: "Come again?"

"Long story short, I ran into this guy in a Waffle House across from where we were staying in Atlanta and he somehow knew who we were and what we were up to. Said that if we wouldn't mind helping him, he'd help us with what we are trying to do. So we go to what turns out to be Faulkner's house, the front door's open, and his signature is there in a guestbook dated fifteen minutes before we get here. Sam Decker, beautifully handwritten."

"You say Sam Decker?"

"Yeah."

"Well I'll be..."

Sunny said, "You know the guy?"

"Not personally."

"He from around here?"

"No, he been in the local news lately. Something to do with horse racin', I don't really know. Let me go get your okra, it's up..."

Over okra and coffee, Sunny and I looked up the local news on Decker. In the Oxford Eagle, we found the following story published by the Eagle's court reporter two months ago:

Spence's first-of-its-kind horse-doping lawsuit tied up in Florida courts, no end in sight

By: Julie Ng,
jng@oxfordeagle.com

A year after filing a first-of-its-kind lawsuit, Benjamin Spence, an Oxford based horse-racing bettor is still waiting to receive $50,000 in the settlement of his claims that he was cheated out of his winnings when a doped horse trained by Tassajara Racing, a California based thoroughbred horse racing operation won a race in Florida in 2017.

After the lawsuit was filed in March 2017, leading figures in horse racing said they had never before heard of such a case, which accused the trainer, an employee of Tassajara's principal Sam Decker, of fraud and racketeering.

The fate of the settlement is still in murky water. Lawyers representing prominent Oxford resident Benjamin Spence have been in extensive negotiations with lawyers representing the lawsuit's two defendants -- trainer

Sallie Jane Holland who is also a co-owner of Tassajara and Sam Decker, the media shy majority owner of Tassajara.

Under the proposed settlement, the defendants are being asked to pay Spence $50,000. Spence has said he'd donate $10,000 of the proposed settlement toward Rowan Oak restoration efforts in wake of continued vandalization.

The proposed settlement would bar the parties from making any future claims related to the case and would stipulate that the agreement would not constitute an admission of liability.

The lawsuit, filed in U.S. District Court in Florida, was financed entirely by the deep pocketed Spence. Spence hopes this first-of-its-kind lawsuit will open the gate for more litigation by bettors hopefully curtailing illegal horse doping. PETA contends that injured horses are sometimes dying on the tracks because they were doped illegally or overmedicated to keep them running when they should be recuperating.

Spence, an experienced self-made gambler, said he hoped the lawsuit would strengthen efforts to "clean up thoroughbred horse-racing."

"We are facing a lot of opposition because of the precedent involved, but I hope this will open the door for others to come forward and hold those responsible accountable for their blatant cheating at tracks across North America," he said in a statement. "Bettors must organize and go after the cheats for every verifiable dime that was lost."

Andrew Peters, one of Decker's lawyers, described the case as "a David vs. Goliath type thing," with Spence able to finance extensive litigation against two defendants who are not prominent figures in horse-racing and have far fewer resources.

"It has been rough for us to defend this case on all fronts because of the amount of money that Spence has poured into it," Peters said. "It shows they had no evidence of criminal wrongdoing or they wouldn't have tried settling so cheaply."

The lawsuit said Spence placed wagers through an online betting site on a race at the Tampa Bay Downs on February 15, 2017. The horses he picked to place first through fourth instead finished behind Tassajara's Zen Master, who had been a long-shot in the race.

Tampa Bay Downs later revealed that Zen Master had tested positive for EPO, a banned performance-enhancing substance, based on blood samples taken in January. As a result, Decker was barred from competing at Tampa Bay Downs, but there was no redress for bettors such as Spence. Decker has adamantly disputed the test results.

"The positive EPO test was planted," said Decker. "We have reams of data and tests that illustrate that Zen Master won fair and square without being doped. This lawsuit is a witch hunt against a new way of training horses perfected at Tassajara. We will continue to fight this case until justice is served. Zen Master and our entire team deserve the win at Tampa Bay Downs."

According to his lawsuit, he correctly picked the horses that finished second, third, fourth and fifth behind the doped horse in various wagers that would have paid a combined $289,835 if Zen Master had been disqualified.

The lawsuit alleged fraud on the part of Holland and the company that owns Zen Master. It also alleged violations of the federal and state anti-racketeering laws known as RICO (Racketeer Influenced and Corrupt Organizations Act), contending that the federal law was violated because Decker was engaging in interstate commerce.

The owner of Tampa Bay Downs, Gary Levinsky, has been among the leaders in horse racing trying to curb doping. The Zen Master doping case emerged through one of his initiatives, establishing "out of competition" drug testing that subjects horses to the possibility of testing at any time.

PETA is critical of thoroughbred horse-racing but is pushing for reforms rather than actively campaigning for an all-out ban.

When our waitress returned with the bill, we asked her about Spence.

"Some love him, others hate him," she said.

"He been around long?"

"Long as I can remember. I been here twenty years and he's tried to do all kinds of things around town. New developments and so on. All from the money he supposedly makes from gambling."

Sunny and I thanked our waitress and left her with a nice tip. By then, we just wanted to get to Memphis and forget about the whole thing. Just too bizarre. Why had Decker reached out to us? Why did he send us to Rowan Oak? It made no sense. The only possible connection we could think of was whether or not Von Rotz somehow knew Decker. Sunny called his mom to see if she'd heard of anyone by that name. Sunny's mom had dated Von Rotz back in the seventies. It was a short lived romance, but they had remained friends all these years later. She had no idea who Decker was. Sunny then asked her if Von Rotz had any recent involvement in horse-racing. No clue, she said. But she did give us an update on his health.

Sadly there were no signs of improvement since telling us of his diagnosis earlier that week. That was only a few days ago though, so I suppose we couldn't expect much.

It took me just over an hour to get us from Oxford to Memphis. There was a cheap Motel 6 on the edge of town that we checked into for the night. The shower I had brought me back to life. Sunny was ready to go for drinks. I was happy to join. But we had to eat barbecue first. Sunny needed a drink before, however. We compromised. One drink at the Peabody, followed by barbecue and then back to the Peabody or straight from barbecue to Beale Street. We took an Uber from the Motel 6. We were dressed to impress. For whatever reason, our spirits were both up. It had been a long, strange day. But I suppose when you arrive in Memphis for the first time and consider all that there is to do, you're bound to have your spirits lifted.

We lucked out with our Uber driver. On our way to the old Grand Dame, he gave us a mini tour. He drove us through the old money part of town and the poor part of town. I asked him where Elvis used to record and he took us to where Sam Phillips' Sun Records recording studio still exists. Far as I was concerned, if you only have time to see one of Sun Records or Graceland, you go to Sun Records. If you want to see the true essence of the birth of the king of rock n' roll, you don't go to Graceland. You go to the place that enabled the excess of Graceland. That place is the recording studio that Sam Phillips founded all those years ago. Sun Records is a magical place. I always thought Graceland represented everything wrong with what happened to Elvis. The celebrity, the money, the excess. To Sunny, you go and see Graceland to see the temple of Elvis. We agreed to disagree. Our driver then dropped us off at Central BBQ. We changed course from going to the Peabody first. That plan was too busy. We were in need of heavy rest. Dislocations from one place to another didn't fit the evening's MO.

From the outside, Central BBQ isn't anything to look at it. Barbecue need not be aesthetic. This isn't Puck territory. This is hole in the wall, substance over style. Sunny and I walked through the rickety screen door and went through the busy family restaurant and out back. The employees wore uniform. Again, nothing fancy. I knew we were in the right spot before we sat down. Sometimes with restaurants, you can just tell. We sat down near live music. Memphis is ground zero for country, blues, rock n' roll, gospel. Each style of music stands on its own in this town and each style is blended. It's melting pot. This kind of urban culture, Sunny and I hadn't seen since New Orleans.

Now, New Orleans compared to Memphis, two different cats. They call New Orleans the big easy. And they do so for good reason. But in Memphis, there's an even slower pace. The music, the food, the people, the Mississippi River: all move a little slower than in Nawlins. Maybe that's because we weren't in Memphis for a special event. We saw New Orleans during one of the city's most significant celebrations. Jazz Fest is the bull moose of North American music festivals. I would go so far as to say that without Jazz Fest pioneering the way, we wouldn't have the Coachella's, Bonaroo's, you name it. Jazz Fest is the progenitor. Anyway, at Central BBQ, Sunny and I sat down in our plastic chairs. We were outside and the warm Memphis air enveloped us. The rains had hit this town too. But now they were gone and what was left was sweet, clean, fresh, rain-washed, particulate-free air. We both put our elbows on the picnic table that had a checkered table cloth. I closed my eyes and exhaled.

"Let's take our time."

"Yes."

"This has been a trip unlike any I've ever been on, will ever be on."

"Yes, me too."

"Let's take our time and eat slow cooked meat on white bread and drink beer."

"Yeah."

"You like this music?"

The music was country. From the country. I'm not talking the slick, Nashville produced chart topper hit parade stuff. I'm talking family-band-from-the-hills music. Strings, mainly. There were five of them. Maybe they were family, maybe not. They looked similar. As a band, they were tightern hell. Mom was playing the mandolin. Dad was rhythm acoustic guitar. The two sons looked like twins. One was on lead guitar, the other was on the jug. The daughter was lead vocal on the box drum. No covers for this band. Well, not to my ear. All the stuff they were playing was old tyme. They were playing originals for all I know, but then they could well have been 19th century standards. The music was what I needed. Even Sunny, Mr. EDM, he was diggin' it.

So we sat at our picnic table and listened. Didn't say a word to one another for a good twenty minutes. We didn't even notice that a server hadn't come by our table. We didn't care. In between each song, we clapped. Not loudly and there was no whistling. Just steady, respectful clapping. The band had a piece of cardboard set up in front of the daughter's box drum. They called themselves Tennessee Mountain Fox Chase.

Noticing their name, only then did it strike me Sunny and I were now in Tennessee. I had missed the big sign on the state line and spaced that we'd crossed into a new state. Some state lines boldly proclaim what state you are now in. Others, not so much. Each time we crossed into Alabama, of course I noticed the giant billboard. *Sweet Home Alabama*. An unresolved question I have is: Did the band come up with that phrase or did the state? Did Van Zant see those same signs I saw, inspiring his song? Or the other way around?

The band took a break and then Sunny and I woke from our mutual trance. I felt like I'd just woken from a nap. A server came by, she said: "Ya'll know ya gotta order at the counter right?"

In we went and waited in the short line to place our food orders. At Central, the saying is: "Smoke is our sauce." I ordered one pulled pork sandwich and one brisket sandwich. Sunny was more conservative. He ordered the pulled pork. The food arrived in no time. I was halfway through the pulled pork when the band started again. I was eating at such a rate that I had two of these big sandwiches sitting in my stomach in less than fifteen minutes. So much for taking my time. God was it good, though with a slice of white bread on the side and a Bud Light to wash it down. I was done my sandwiches in the same time it took Sunny to eat his one.

A note on barbecue: In the US, barbecue is regional. Certain regions have different methods to cook and present the meat. Whether you're in Charleston, Austin, Kansas City or Memphis, the common denominator is that meat is cooked slow. For hours and hours, it's cooked. In Memphis, hickory and pecan woods are used as fuel for the fire. The Memphis tradition of barbecue emphasizes pork and use of dry rub. In central Texas, brisket is more famous. And in Texas, these big slabs of beef are cooked in pits in the ground. The Carolinas are more about pork on a spit. And then there's Kansas City barbecue, famous for pork and the heaping spoonfuls of liberally applied sauce. Tomato and molasses-based sauces are the norm. Great sauce in Kansas City. Of course, there are barbecue purists that will dispute what I am saying. I'm giving you the broad strokes. If you want to get molecular, you can find variation everywhere. Sure there are differences between west, east, central and south Texas barbecue. But in discussing barbecue, there's a difference between scratching your ass and tearing it to bits.

And there's no such thing as a Best Barbecue. It's not a competition, despite plenty of competitions across the country. To me, food should not be about that. To organize a food competition is missing the point entirely. Leave the compete factor for the track, the rink, the court. After our foot race, then we go eat like kings together and forget about that nasty business of competition, if only for a little while. That's my personal opinion. Of course, Sunny thinks differently. He doesn't see why there can't be competitions in food. Sunny said, "Why not? Why are you so damn rigid about this stuff?" I just am. Tennessee Mountain Fox Chase played on. I was hoping I'd get a chance to speak to one of them to hear their story. How and where and why and who? I like that a family like that can exist in this world. But on that night, it wasn't for me to know.

Sunny and I rolled out of the restaurant. We were so unbelievably full. Me much more than him. The pains started pretty quick on our way to the Peabody. My stomach could not process it all. I was being punished. My taste buds had sabotaged my stomach. By the time Sunny and I got to the Peabody, I was hunched over. I couldn't stand up straight. I was in such pain from the barbecue. It was horrible. Sunny thought I was pathetic. "Drink with me," he said as we walked into the old Peabody. This was quite the hotel. It's ancient, opulent, grand, excessive and...it fits. The place just works. They sure knew how to build hotels back in the day. Back when I can only assume Memphis had more going for it. These days, poverty is rampant and jobs are disappearing. Unlike Atlanta or Nashville, Memphis hasn't seen much in the way of economic growth in recent decades. In Memphis, there's lots to be blue about. But then you have sparkling points of civic pride like the Peabody. That grand dame of a hotel is from another time and place. If you want charm, elegance, gracious hospitality, you go to the Peabody. If you want to see a daily occurrence of five ducks marching through the lobby first at eleven in the morning and then at five at night, you go to the Peabody. And if you want finely crafted cocktails, you go straight to the Peabody's Lobby Bar.

At the Lobby Bar, Sunny and I posted up. Sunny ordered a peach sour while I tried navigating a cacophony of good choice from the drinks menu. All the while, feeling incredible pain in my stomach. Our bartender could see the pain on my face.

She said, "You need a John Collins."

"Because?"

"Because you ate too much food for dinner."

"What about the..."

"John Collins."

"But how do you know?"

"Why do you doubt me?"

"Okay then. I'll have a John Collins." Talking was difficult. I was in serious pain. Sunny was frustrated with my operatic behaviour.

"Some drinkin' partner you are."

"Give me a minute. She'll be right, mate."

I was soon on the way to the nearest restroom. I had to try and fix this. Never before had I ever tried forcing food out of my mouth that I'd already eaten. But in the men's restroom, I did just that. I don't want to go into details. But there I was, on my knees, with my index finger down my throat. Ugly business. I was battling away in that restroom for a good fifteen minutes. Did it work? I wish I could say it did. After lord knows how many attempts, I was too exhausted to continue. Central BBQ won. I was bent over, resting both arms on the toilet seat, head hanging off the side, knees banged up off the immaculate marble flooring, gasping away, spitting out bile. And then I heard footsteps.

I was distracted by my condition. I didn't give it much thought that I was now in a position to embarrass myself. I tried to keep quiet as I continued to writhe in stomach pain. There was no end in sight to this. From where I was strewn across the restroom floor, I could see two snakeskin loafers pointed directly in the direction of my stall from across the room. Whoever had now joined me in there clearly didn't need to use the facilities. The stranger just stood there a moment as if to wait to see if I would react to his presence. Must be hotel staff, I concluded. I called out, "I'm okay, just need a minute." Snakeskin didn't reply. Instead, he threw something toward me that slid underneath my stall. His throw was right on the mark. It was a small Waffle House to-go bag. "Thank you," I called out. Again, no reply. And just like that, there was no one else in the restroom. "Hello? Anyone there?" Nothing. Inside was a single waffle. I ate it in a few short bites, and crumpled up in my pocket the waffle's wrapping.

As I made my return to the bar, I could see Sunny was in fine form. Here was a handsome old devil putting in work. In the half hour I was gone, my chair had been usurped by a rather striking blonde. The bartender saw me approach and smiled as if to say she knew the dynamic. She pointed to the John Collins she'd saved for me behind the bar. I didn't want to interrupt Sundance, so I took a seat at the end of the bar. He didn't notice my return because his back was turned from me. The bartender introduced herself. Jo gave me my John Collins. She said, "You need this. Where've you been? Your friend thought you'd left to Beale or something. Said you have that kind of a tendency."

"Oh, do I now? Thanks for saving my drink."

"Well, this one I actually just made for myself. Your pal already drank the one you'd ordered."

"Well thanks for giving me your drink."

"It'll help. Trust me."

"So will that waffle, I hope," I said as I flashed Jo the wrapping. "You tell one of your colleagues I was in there? Had some pretty flashy shoes from my vantage point." Jo was busy taking orders on a busy Wednesday evening. "What was that, hun?"

"Did you tell someone I was in there? I had Waffle House thrown to me while I was trying to...did you tell anyone?

"Nope. Maybe he did?"

"Sunny did?"

"I don't know, ask him."

"He's preoccupied."

"Has been for a while now. I can't say I think he missed you."

"May I please make an order?"

"Go right ahead."

"I'll have another one of these and I'd like to also order Sunny and his new friend another round too."

"Sure thing."

Jo served my drink first and then handed Sunny and Blondie their drinks. They both just took them without thinking about who may have ordered them. Jo looked over at me shaking my head in disbelief. I said, "Can you believe this guy?" He was oblivious to the world around him. Jo laughed and shrugged.

She said, "She is a looker though, you gotta admit."

"Can I ask you something?"

"Depends."

"Oh, please. I'm not like that."

"Like what?" Jo was teasing.

"Nevermind."

"What did you want to ask?"

"What shoes you got on?"

"Why does that matter?"

"It doesn't. I'm just curious."

"What they give me's all."

"Who?"

"The Peabody."

"You got uniform?"

"Yeah, all of us do."

"You mean, you have to wear the shoes that the Peabody gives you?"

"This wasn't what I thought you were going to ask me. Yes, they do."

"What happens if you don't wear uniform?"

"They won't let us work."

"That strict?"

"Yes. Now, may I ask why you're so curious about my shoes?"

"Well, I'm just wondering who the guy was in the restroom who threw me the Waffle House. He was wearing snakeskin loafers."

"Wouldn't have been staff, that's for sure. No supervisor would let anyone of us wear something like that."

"That right, eh?"

"You got any other friends here? Hang on." Jo was being summoned. Meanwhile, Sunny was still at work. I had had enough. At least the guy could show some respect for a drink on the house.

"Hey Sunny!" I yelled from across the bar. He looked up, unaware of who or where his name was called from. "You're wife called, askin' where you been all night." Sunny whirled around. Blondie instantly went for it.

"Meko? How long you been there?"

"You...have a wife?" Blondie said. Sunny turned back around to his sparring partner. She was now standing. She didn't look too happy.

"No, no, no. That's just my cousin, he's just kiddin' around...hey where you going? Wait, Gina, don't go..why you gotta..."

"I don't mess around with married men, lonesome Harry's, whatever it is you are."

"Oh yeah?" What about that ring on your finger..huh?"

"You mean this one?" Gina said, holding her right hand up. She had a ring on her pinky finger.

"Yeah that one," Sunny said.

"You're something else, you know that? I'm outta here." And she was. Just like that, Gina was gone. Sunny looked over at me.

"Why'd you gotta do that, you sonnuvabitch? We were getting along!"

"Yeah well, thanks for checking how I was doing in there. For all you know, I coulda been in the hospital by now!"

"Buddy eats a little too much at dinner and thinks he needs to go to the hospital."

Jo came to my defence: "You know Gina's in here every night, just sayin'..."

"What do you mean? Said she was from the East coast visiting with her folks."

Jo said, "That what she said this time?"

"What do you mean?"

"Last night, she was in from Atlanta on business. Night before that, she was in town for the vet conference..."

"You're serious..."

"Sorry, hun."

"Well, shit," Sunny said, looking at the drinks I ordered for him.

"Ever cross your mind where those came from?"

"Didn't I order...you got these for me?"

"You guys wanna sit together and quit yelling across my bar, please? Thank you."

We apologized to Jo and I went back to the seat that had been occupied by Miss Gina. It was toasty warm.

Sunny and I drank one more for the road, paid up and left. Sunny's bill, which included Gina's many espresso martinis, was as grand as the Peabody itself. As we made our way to the exit, I pretended as if I'd forgotten something at the bar. "Be right back," I said to Sunny. "Forgot to leave a tip." I went back not to leave a tip. I'd already done that. I had to know one thing. Jo saw me from afar. Before I could even ask, she said: "I've never seen that woman in my life." She was referring to Gina. What I thought. "Thanks, anyone ever says there's nothing much to being a bartender. I'll send them your way."

Sunny was waiting for me outside. The air was still fresh from rainfall. A perfect spring night in southern Tennessee. There was one more thing on our evening itinerary. Beale Street. From the Peabody, it's only a few blocks to that famous stretch of street. It was much smaller than I'd imagined. I wasn't sure why I thought it would be bigger. It did certainly live up to its reputation for being a bastion of bluesy live music. Every single bar and there are lots, had a live band ripping away at some cover tune. There were a few originals here and there, but it was mainly covers of music most Americans are familiar with.

Beale Street runs all the way from downtown Memphis to the banks of the Mississippi. Sunny and I couldn't exactly tell that was the case because between where we stood on Beale Street's west end and where the road ends at the banks of the river, the street was packed with people. Hundreds of people, all on motorcycles, and they were all black. It may be hard to picture, but that was the scene. The entirety of Beale Street was as tightly packed as a can of sardines with black motorcyclists in black leather.

How odd, how cool was this? And it wasn't exactly a kumbaya group of bikers. There was plenty of trash talk and rowdiness. I don't think it would be accurate to say what we were looking at was a massive biker gang. It came across more as a sort of club meeting. But it was nothing like we'd ever seen before. The hundreds of Harley's howled away in concert with remnant screams of street corner Stratocasters. Sunny tried asking the nearest biker what the deal was. He was too far into the drink to give us an answer. I was still in pain from gorging on the barbecue. Not as much as before, as the Waffle House and Jo's drink recommendation did help, but it was still there. This was much to the annoyance of Sunny. I took out the Waffle House wrapping, which I'd forgotten to tell Sunny about until then. We went to King's Palace Cafe, sat down with an outward view of Beale and ordered beer.

Sunny: "Waffle House? How? When?"

"You have no idea."

"Where'd you get that?"

After telling Sunny about my visit from Snakeskin, he just nodded his head as if to say, yeah that shouldn't have happened. All of his follow up questions, I'd already considered. He and I had the same amount of information. We came to the same conclusion. Probably had something to do with our man Decker.

"You think he's in town?"

"Don't know."

"How would he know we were at the Peabody?"

"Don't know."

"What the hell was that stunt about anyway him pulling that guestbook trick?"

"Don't know. Anything you ask, I can almost guarantee I'll say I don't know."

"So strange. Where's more Waffle House when you need it."

"What do you mean?"

"For your stomach. You need more."

"You think eating more Waffle House would help my digestion?"

"At this point, why would it be wrong to think otherwise?"

"Good point."

"You wanna see if we can find one?"

"As much as I think it may actually help, the answer is no. I can't think about food right now. I can't even look at it. No more food. In fact, when our beers get here, you have mine all right? I'll order a whiskey or something instead."

"Ok and what about tomorrow?"

"What about tomorrow."

"Where we going? I don't know about you, but I haven't even thought about it till now."

"Gina, helluva girl."

"She sure got me. Wow."

"Yeah, quite the act."

"Anyway, where to tomorrow?"

The server brought us our beer, I ordered a shot of Jack on ice and before he went back to his bar, Sunny asked about what was happening on Beale. Our server said that this particular roundup happens every month. This group of bikers, they come from all over the city, state and beyond. "Welcome to Memphis," he said. "And don't worry, they're not looking for any trouble." We didn't last long in that bar. The band was playing too many bad Stevie Ray Vaughan covers. Nothing against Stevie. The guy was a guitar genius who could sing. Stevie cover bands just don't often work for that reason alone. We left after our drinks and walked all the way to the river. As we walked, we narrowed the choice for our next destination to either St. Louis or Nashville. It didn't take long for us to settle on Nashville. There was lots to see in Music City and it was one less hour on the road. Sunny and I agreed, more time out of the car was for the better at this point in the trip.

NOVEMBER 12

Dear Lula Mae,

Well, we made it. I write this letter to you from an old Victorian town-house in the heart of San Francisco. We're staying at a friend of Meko's in the central Western Addition neighbourhood. Our Victorian is on Fulton Street, which runs alongside Alamo Square Park's north side. Alamo Square is known for its views of the city looking north and for the row of restored Victorians known as the Painted Ladies. Those houses are iconic San Francisco imagery and they abut the park.

There are plenty of people that go to Alamo Square for no other reason than to gaze at the Painted Ladies. Many people know of them from post-cards or from the opening credits to that old TV show *Full House*. People live in those houses. I would not enjoy living in a house with a steady stream of locals and tourists from all over the world staring at my front door. Everyday. Odd, don't you think? The Painted Ladies are on Steiner Street, which runs north-south on the park's eastern side. There's also a dog park on the west side of Alamo Square. Meko and I have been going there daily.

Have you been to this city before? I'm in love with it. It's early Novem-ber, but it feels like summer. The sun is out, the humidity is low, tempera-tures are perfect. I've been told fall is the best time to visit this part of California. I would've thought the summer months, but no, they say fall takes the cake. San Franciscans renamed August, Fogust. I think the San Francisco climate is the one for me. It's never too hot, nor too cold. It's easy to live in. Unlike the freezing north, you don't think twice about the weather if an urge to go for an evening stroll hits you at ten at night, mid-November.

There's activity in this town. It's buzzing. The best of everything is here. Food, drink, music, art, work, the list goes on. But they sure don't give this place away. Rent is through the roof. Not just rent but everything. It's worth it, I'm convinced. Sure, you can live comfortably for a quarter of the price in Podunk, but then, so far as I'm aware, do we not only get one ticket on this ride of life? Make no mistake, San Francisco has a dark side. The homeless problem is out of control. There are gangs. There are drugs. There is a lot of bad. But the positives about this place outweigh the negatives by a long shot.

Near the Western Addition is the Panhandle. The Panhandle is a narrow urban park that eventually joins with the giant Golden Gate Park. Both are just the best for runs. Treed, grassy, shady, just the best. Golden Gate Park runs all the way west to Ocean Beach. I'm telling you, it's huge. There are museums in there, botanical gardens, bison paddocks, tracks, lakes, polo fields, golf courses, disc golf courses, picnic areas, Japanese tea gardens, academies of science, nurseries, stadiums, tennis courts, soccer fields, flower conservatories, Dutch windmills and I'm sure I'm forgetting what else. Oh, and big music festivals take place in there too.

Before I get carried away on San Francisco, let me just sum up how the rest of our Pacific Coast road trip went. From Mendocino down Highway 1 along the windy coast, it took us about half a day of comfortable driving to arrive in the city. What a gorgeous drive along the California coast. Manchester, Sea Ranch, Timber Cove, Bodega Bay and then Point Reyes until arriving at Bolinas. We had a snack at tiny Bolinas and were told by our barista to check out nearby Mt. Tamalpais and the Muir Woods. We hiked up Mt. Tam and then explored the Redwoods of Muir Woods. From the summit of Mt. Tam, there are panoramic views of the city to the south. We could see the city's skyline and the Golden Gate Bridge that would take us there.

Marin County is the land on the north side of the bridge. It's country. Van Morrison territory. Apparently, he lives somewhere up there. I can see why. I like Marin County a lot. You're away from the busy city, but it's a short drive over an iconic bridge to get there if need be. We went through seaside Sausalito last before going over the iconic bridge. We had sunny weather. We lucked out. Next thing, we were driving through the Presidio and then there we were in the heart of San Francisco.

It was quite the road trip. We saw lots, did lots, learned lots. I was on the receiving end of quite the yarn, the Run For Roses, which I will detail later. I don't even know the ending yet. Meko got as far as explaining the Nashville part of the trip and then we arrived in the city. He said I would have to wait until we left for the Rocky Mountains of Utah and Colorado for the grand finale. What's in the Rockies, you may wonder? Lord knows. He did mention a friend of his, Jack Badenhausen, he needed to visit for work. And if you're wondering, I don't blame you. No, we haven't yet travelled south toward Carmel. I don't know if we will or not. I also don't know how long we are going to be spending in SF. Meko said, could be a week, could be a month. The room we have to stay in, it's small, like really small. It's basically a closet. But we don't need any more room. Days and nights are spent out and about.

On nearby Divisadero Street, there's a barbecue joint Meko frequents often. He says it's on par with the Memphis barbecue he waxed poetic about in that last letter. Though he's learned his lesson. He takes his time eating it. Sometimes he has leftovers for me. It's otherworldly good. The other restaurant I want to write about is the breakfast spot on the corner of Fulton and Divis. Eddie's. This is the place. It's small. It's owned by South Koreans. Breakfast comfort food is served. Pancakes and eggs and toast. It's affordable. It's a San Francisco rarity.

Most cafes, breakfast joints in this town are of the $10 toast, $7 latte variety. Expensive and *so* cool. Designer. Not Eddie's. It stands on its own. You walk through the doors, on weekends there is always a line, and you are transported back to McQueen's SF. Eddie's was founded as a typical soul food cafe. The hard working South Korean family that runs it, they haven't changed it one bit. The menu is the same. Prices may be a little higher, but only just a little. And they're so kind. Eddie's...you gotta go. The Western Addition used to primarily be a black neighbourhood. That was before the tidal wave of San Francisco gentrification hit. Tech workers in town, and there are lots, there's love for their spending and sales tax contributions. There's also lots of resentment toward them.

It's nothing personal, so far as I'm aware. If you're a fifth-generation San Franciscan social worker and now you can't afford to live where you and your parents and your grandparents grew up, I would be angry too. Mr. Google, Mrs. Facebook, are being paid double, triple, quadruple you are, and commute two hours to work each morning to their South Bay office. Many inner city SF neighbourhoods are bedroom communities serving corporate campus Silicon Valley. So far, I've walked my way through the following areas: Cow Hollow, Pacific Heights, Russian Hill, Telegraph Hill, Nob Hill, North Beach, Embarcadero, Polk, SOMA, Financial District, Chinatown, Japantown, Haight-Ashbury, Duboce, Presidio Heights and the Castro. I've logged a few miles. Went out to the Cliff House the other day too. I have yet to go down to the Mission. I have no desire to see Alcatraz. The Dogpatch is still on my to-do list. So is Noe Valley.

The places I've visited, they all have their good and bad. For example, Fisherman's Wharf is just too touristy. But it's also home to Ghirardelli's chocolate. I have yet to take a chance in the Tenderloin. Meko and I were in an Uber one day and the driver said that he'd never take a chance picking up or dropping off in the Tenderloin at night. Specifically the intersection of Turk and Hyde. It's a scary part of the city. I found the following description in a newspaper article to illustrate:

The heroin needles, the pile of excrement between parked cars, the yellow soup oozing out of a large plastic bag by the curb and the stained, faux Persian carpet dumped on the corner.

It's a scene of detritus that might bring to mind any variety of developing-world squalor. But this is San Francisco, the capital of the nation's technology industry, where a single span of Hyde Street hosts an open-air narcotics market by day and at night is occupied by the unsheltered and drug-addled slumped on the sidewalk.

There are many other streets like it, but by one measure, it's the dirtiest block in the city.

Just a 15-minute walk away are the offices of Twitter and Uber, two companies that along with other nameplate technology giants have helped push the median price of a home in San Francisco well beyond $1 million.

This dichotomy of street crime and world-changing technology, of luxury condominiums and grinding, persistent homelessness, and the dehumanizing effects for those forced to live on the streets provoke outrage among the city's residents. For many who live here it's difficult to reconcile San Francisco's liberal politics with the misery that surrounds them.

Like I said, San Francisco is far from perfect. But really, is there such a place...anywhere? I don't think so. But I'll keep looking. What's Meko up to here? Wish I could tell you. He's not saying much. He'll leave for a few hours at a time and return. He says he's working on stories. He also said he's started working on his first ever novel. He's dating a girl down here. Maybe that's why we made the trip. Work serves for many as worthy cover for alternative intention. They went to a Willie Nelson concert the other night over in Oakland at the Fox Theater. The Red Headed Stranger is in his late eighties and he still sells out one of the Bay Area's best venues. Willie is a national treasure. On and on he went about that concert. I guess things are progressing well with the girl. I'll report back when I know more. Like what her name is. I'm meeting her today and three of her friends.

It's early on a Saturday morning. I wanted to write this to you and the Nashville part of Run For Roses before leaving for Marin County for the day. Meko's girl is organizing. Tucked away on the side of Mt.Tam, over-looking Muir Woods, is the German Tourist Club. Usually private, some-how we have access. What I know so far: Winding roads lead to a parking lot, which leads to a quarter-mile hike through the woods to a century old Bavarian lodge with a view to die for.

And yes, German beer is served.

Love always,
Foxworth

* * *

How Sunny and Meko learned to give themselves permission on certain aspects of travel while in Nashville; what a true honky-tonk can be; and what family-style dining can do for the soul

Neither Sunny nor I had ever been to Nashville before arriving there mid-morning on Thursday, May 3rd, 2018. Nashville's tourism brand is strong. As first-timers, we felt a sort of obligation, like we did with Mem-phis, toward checking out the pillars of Nashville tourism.

Before we checked into our hotel, motel, Airbnb, or hostel, we went straight to the Grand Ole Opry. It wasn't even lunch hour when we pulled up to the place located far from Nashville's commercial core. Why go to the Opry late morning on a Thursday? Because we felt we had to. There was no other time to visit the country music institution. Sunny and I formulated an ad hoc Nashville itinerary as we drove north from Memphis. In keeping with the Von Rotzian free-wheelin' spirit, we kept it pretty loose. In our minds, it probably looked something like this:

1. Opry
2. Hotel
3. Exercise
4. Food
5. Wander
6. Cocktail
7. Food
8. Broadway
9. Sleep
10. Breakfast
11. Wander
12. Leave

Pretty simple. Visiting the Opry without a show to go to was a hollow experience. The only thing that sticks with me was finding a book in the gift shop about country music songwriters explaining the how and why of their iconic songs. In that book, there was a passage from Jerry Jeff Walker explaining how his magnificent Mr. Bojangles came to be. To paraphrase: Jerry Jeff was an unknown bar singer in New Orleans when he thought of the song. It was the middle 1960's. One night, he was thrown in a drunk tank to cool off. In the cell that night, he met a homeless New Orleans street performer. The performer had been arrested as part of a police sweep of poor people following a murder. Mr. Bojangles was not his real name. The man made it up when the police arrested him.

Jerry Jeff and Bojangles talked about all kinds of things that night. When Bojangles told a story about his dog dying, one of the other cellmates asked for something more uplifting. Bojangles obliged with a tap dance. The man took his pseudonym from Bill "Bojangles" Robinson. The actual Bojangles was the best known and highest earning black American entertainer in America during the first half of the 20th century. Jerry Jeff Walker had his narrative. But what about the lyric structure? Enter Dylan Thomas. At the time, he was reading a lot of Thomas and was inspired to incorporate internal rhyme into his lyrics.

The result:

I knew a man Bojangles and he'd dance for you in worn out shoes
Silver hair, ragged shirt and baggy pants, that old soft shoe
He'd jump so high, he'd jump so high, then he lightly touched down
Mr. Bojangles, Mr. Bojangles, dance.

I met him in a cell in New Orleans, I was down and out
He looked to me to be the eyes of age as he spoke right out
He talked of life, he talked of life, laughing slapped his leg stale
Mr. Bojangles, Mr. Bojangles, dance.

He said the name Bojangles and he danced a lick all across the cell
He grabbed his pants for a better stance, oh, he jumped so high and he clicked his heels
He let go a laugh, he let go a laugh, shook back his clothes all around
Mr. Bojangles, Mr. Bojangles, dance, yeah, dance.

He danced for those at minstrel shows and county fairs
throughout the south
He spoke with tears of 15 years of how his dog and him
but just travelled all about
His dog up and died, he up and died, and after 20 years he still grieves

Mr. Bojangles, Mr. Bojangles, dance.

He said, "I dance now at every chance at honky-tonks for drinks and tips.
But most of the time I spend behind these county bars, 'cause I drinks a bit'"
He shook his head, yes, he shook his head, I heard someone ask him, "Please,
Mr. Bojangles, Mr. Bojangles, dance, dance, Mr. Bojangles, dance."

The hostel we found was everything we needed. It was the best place we stayed for our entire southern sojourn. New, cheap, clean, young, and close to Broadway. If you're ever in Nashville, stay at the Nashville Downtown Hostel. True to its marketing, it's steps away from the honky tonk capital of the world. And it's across the street from the Cumberland River, the big river that runs through the heart of the city.

Sunny and I got a four bed dorm room. There was another guy already checked in. We met him as we dropped our things off. Some people stick with you. There was something about this guy. He was so plain. His clothes were plain. His face was plain. His mannerisms were plain. Everything about him was plain. Even his luggage. We said our hellos. His name was Cyrus. He was just passing through and was on his way out the door to do some sightseeing. He left a plain bible on his pillow. I don't why, something about the guy just sticks in my memory.

After all the driving and eating and drinking, I needed to exercise. Sunny felt the same way. We go about exercising in different ways. I am a runner. Sunny lifts weights. He was in luck. The hostel had a few dumb-bells lying around. To warm-up, he joined me on the first bit of my run before turning back to do pushups and curls and so on.

My run through Nashville consisted of first going down to the Cumberland River pathway system and running north into Germantown. In Germantown, I saw brewpub after brewpub. I returned south and went over the Woodland Street bridge into East Nashville. This looked like Nashville's equivalent to what Frenchman Street is to Bourbon Street in New Orleans. I finished at the state capitol. Running through a new city is up there for one of my favourite activities. Endorphins are flowing and you're seeing new terrain. When I got back to the hostel, I was a new man. I felt great and what's more, Sunny and I had a night on the town ahead of us. I caught up to Sunny in the hostel's common area. Even though it was mid-afternoon, plenty of the hostel's guests had started their imbibing. This is hostel culture in a party town. What I didn't realize however, was that there was also playoff hockey happening. I didn't know Nashville was such a hockey town. Albertan Sunny was in his element.

Now, you may be wondering how I have a Canadian cousin. Until now, I haven't bothered filling you in on this detail. In the 1980s, my mom's sister Ruthie answered an ad in Town and Country magazine. The ad, and apparently this was a thing, maybe still is, was a guy looking for a partner. Ruthie answered the ad, unaware that the guy was a Canadian. They met on their first date in Whitefish, Montana. They fell in love. It was straight out of a Debbie Macomber novel. Sunny's dad took his new love back home to his family's ranch near a little town in the southern Alberta foothill. It's called Longview and it has long views of the Rocky Mountains to the west that are just incredible. Growing up, I would visit twice per year. Once in the summer to fly fish, and once in the winter to ski Lake Louise or Fernie. The skiing in that part of Canada is much better than in Taos, where I grew up skiing.

The Nashville Predators had a big home playoff game the night we arrived in town. Bonus for us. Visiting a city when the home team is in a deep playoff run is a good idea. We thought about trying to snag a couple tickets, but the prices were just too high from the online scalpers. We had other things to see anyway. Wherever we would eat and drink, we'd listen to music and watch the game. I'm not really a hockey fan, but it is fun to watch. More fun than golf, anyway.

By the time we reached Nashville, New Orleans felt like a lifetime ago. It's safe to say that I was already a different person, having made it this far in our trip. I think I can speak for Sunny and say the same had happened to him. We'd come along way. We'd seen a lot, done a lot, met some wild people, had some otherworldly experiences.

In the hostel, we met a lot of our fellow travellers. Most were there to see all the same stuff. But some were there to start their musical careers. They'd travelled from all over to be the next big thing in country music. There were more than a few people we met who blankly told us they had just moved here to pursue their dream of becoming a musician. Who knew, Sunny and I may have been talking to the next Toby Keith, Taylor Swift. They worshipped at the altar of places like the Bluebird Cafe. The little places the songwriter set go to test their wares and hopefully be noticed. If that's what you love to do, all the power to you. Tough way to make a living. The buskers in Nashville, like New Orleans, all have chops. They are all outstanding musicians. Few will make it, though. It's a competitive business, music. But there's a lot of people in the world. And can you think of anyone who doesn't like music? As a budding musician, you can at least can rest easy knowing you have a market of billions of people open to what you're selling. Everyone likes music.

We found Nashville to be a groovy little town. Tom T. Hall was right. There were still a few mysteries that needed attending to, Decker and such, but we'd get there. In due time. Sunny had been playing Tom all the way from Memphis. What else did we listen to? There was some Charlie Rich, George Jones, Dolly of course, Conway Twitty, Loretta Lynn, Chet Atkins. I wanted some of that old Nashville. I wanted the polished, produced stuff. I wanted to know what Willie and Waylon acted out against. Some of it ain't that bad. My theory is the outlaw country guys got turned off from Nashville, not so much for the sound, although I am sure there was that too, but more because they hadn't been selected by the Nashville powers that be. The suits. Nashville's musical landscape today is much different than yesteryear. Now you've got artists like Jack White, Dan Auerbach, Alison Mosshart who call Nashville home. There is considerable distance between Conway Twitty and Jack White.

And I have to say that Sunny's approach to music had become much more flexible since we started our trip. It was character development that warmed my heart. As far as me, I'm not sure what kind of character development I'd undergone. That's something you'll need to ask Sunny. That is, if you're curious. When the clock struck five, Sunny and I found ourselves rambling our way down capitol mall state park. Our thirst and appetite had returned. Not even a full twenty-four hours had gone by since I'd proclaimed to Sunny that I'd never eat food again. Yet there I was, ready to once again eat. We could've gone to somewhere like Hattie B's for hot chicken, but we didn't. Somewhere easy, close and without tourist hype. I spoke earlier about the gravitational pull toward aspects of a place with a strong tourism brand. I can also say there are times when after going through those motions, like we'd done earlier in the day, eventually you don't feel the urge. I think this comes with experience as a traveller. Giving ourselves permission to not go to Hattie B's despite feeling obliged, and instead choosing something more immediate and convenient, far less well known, arriving there takes experience. Or laziness. Either way, that's what we did, go elsewhere.

One of the best pleasures of travel are the unpredictable surprises. The things that come from seemingly nowhere, from parts unplanned. The place we found to settle into for a few hours, they had a resident piano man there that blew our socks off. Sometimes he would play and sing solo, and then he'd do a set with his bandmates that would materialize from the bar's woodwork. Sunny and I sat there, can't even remember the name of the place, completely blown away by this guy. He must be headed somewhere. But where is somewhere? With each passing year, it's a question hard to answer. For example, on 60 Minutes the other night, there was a segment about a study of people in their nineties. A group of people who have made it that far and who are in good health (mind and body) check in every six months to test their cognition. The study has been going on for a few years. Scientists have unearthed ground-breaking insights into understanding neurodegenerative diseases like dementia. One of the scientists even said that with where our world is at now, half the babies born today in the United States will make it to one-hundred years old.

Anyway, the real takeaway, the way 60 Minutes ended the segment, was by noting that although considerable advancements have been made, with every question answered, six new questions arise. As in, despite the progress, they seem to know less and less each year! It's a paradox. I bring this up because I can relate that feeling to my approach toward understanding the world through travel. Where will our piano man go? Where's his destination? Is it stardom? What is stardom, anyway? Is it nothing more than byproduct of a bygone industry? Spotify's Top 50 for the United States has less cultural currency than ever if you listen to people like Bob Lefsetz. A rock star, a movie star, in the 1970s had far more power and visibility than those of today. Sure, Drake or Billie tunes can stream billions of times, but do they get through to the masses like peak Elvis? Can a Beatlemania ever happen again? Media is fragmented. In any event, our piano man, wherever he's going, at least he showed up that night to evidence his own humanity - the true mark of good music.

We were also lucky that our attention wasn't diverted by the hockey game. The bar didn't have TV's strewn across the walls. The bar was bucking convention. Live music came first. But when we finished our food and drink, we felt we needed to see how Nashville does hockey. Sunny, of course, is well versed in the culture of hockey. In Canada, hockey is ubiquitous. It's football in America, soccer in Britain, skiing in Austria. Sunny's de facto team is the Calgary Flames. Sunny's not really a puck, but he'll watch the game with the boys back home. It's an unavoidable experience. Sunny played his share of ODR growing up. ODR is Outdoor Rink. To play some ODR, you just go to the community rink with skates, a stick and find a pickup game to join. Through the years on my visits, I gradually learned to skate. Eventually, I was good enough to start ODR'ing. Hockey is a great game. Much better to play than to watch, like all sports.

Walking down Broadway, we looked for a place to watch hockey. The street had transformed from earlier in the light of day when I was on my run. Now it was neon. It was Beale Street but bigger and much rowdier. It didn't have the local chapter of whatever you call that biker squad we stumbled across, but it had all kinds of people from all over. Nashville has become a popular destination to do bachelor, bachelorette parties. Sunny and I saw plenty of tiara's that night. Plenty of protective girlfriends without any interest in vacating the crew.

Bridgestone Arena, where the Predators play, abuts Broadway's west end. The east end is the Cumberland River. There are four blocks of honky tonk in between. That night there was a sea of yellow and white jerseys. At this stage in the NHL Playoffs, the Predators were in the Western Conference Final. The tournament's semi-final. They were playing the Winnipeg Jets. That Winnipeg made it this far surprised Sunny. Sunny is a casual league observer. He is aware of which teams are meant to go far and which ones aren't. Nashville has been a strong club in recent years. The year before, they made it as far as the Stanley Cup Final. They lost to Sidney Crosby's Penguins in six games. For a long time, the Predators have been horrid. As for Winnipeg, only a few years had gone by since Manitoba's capital finally got a franchise. There used to be a team in Winnipeg, but that was from before Sunny and I were in grade school.

The Preds won that night, two to one. The best of seven serious was now even at two games each. The party was on. Sunny and I caught the third period in a Broadway sports bar. It was electric. That same bar had a rooftop. We went there after the win, somehow managing to beat the queue. The view up there was stunning of the surrounding skyline. Sunny was busy getting us drinks while I was chatting up what turned out to be mostly a local's hangout. People asked where I was from. I said my cousin and I were visiting Nashville for the first time from Calgary. I didn't bother telling the drunkards about Arroyo Seco. They would have no idea. Arroyo Seco is a different planet compared to Nashville's Broadway on a Thursday night after a playoff hockey win. Calgary is much nearer and dearer.

Said one: "Love the Flames! Great club."

"Thanks," I said. What else could I say? "We're rebuilding."

If you're a club that doesn't make the playoffs, you're rebuilding. Always rebuilding. The Edmonton Oilers, having missed the playoffs repeatedly despite getting like six first overall draft picks in a row: rebuilding.

Sunny came up with a pitcher of beer. The drunk guy saw him approach and correctly assumed he was my cousin. He said, "You're from Calgary?"

"I am!"

"Where all the Canadian teams this year?" The guy referred to how, of the seven Canadian NHL teams, only two had made it to the Stanley Cup playoffs. A disgrace for the country. The Leafs made it in, but of course, didn't make it past the first round.

"Rebuilding," Sunny said.

"Predators are mostly Canadian anyway," he said.

"Of course. Didn't know Nashville was such a hockey town?"

"Oh yeah, better believe it."

"Since when?"

"Since the only other pro sports team here is the Titans."

"That's it, I guess?"

"We have MLS, but it's still small."

"How the Titans doing?"

"Not good."

"Did Nashville come out like this before the Preds got good?"

"No way."

"Will they in five years if they're where the Flames are now?"

"Good question. One of our owners is from there, you know."

"Who's that?"

"Brett Wilson."

Sunny and the guy were going off on hockey. I needed air. Just as I was leaving, Sunny said: "By the way, saw your buddy Decker!"

"You what?"

"Yeah, he's by the bar. In those snakeskins."

"Sunny, really?"

"No, I'm only kidding. I don't even know what he looks like, remember? Only you've seen him and those snakeskin loafers. All I know, you're yankin' my chain bout all this. Anyway, text where you are."

A sports bar after the game is only good for so long. I left and texted Sunny I was going to find our next bar - a true honky tonk. I walked by Luke Bryan's 32 Bridge, no thanks. Kid Rock's Big Ass Honky Tonk Rock N' Roll Steakhouse...nope. Then I saw Robert's Western World. Wasn't this the boot store I ran by earlier? Yes it was. At night, it transforms into what looked to be a true honky tonk - so far as that is possible on glitzy Broadway.

Robert's Western World is small. It was packed when I got there. Plenty of boots, buckles, blue jeans, plaid, Stetsons and Predators jerseys. After seeing the piano man earlier, I didn't think I'd get any better live music. I was wrong. In Robert's, here was just one more lights out band. These guys were playing mostly covers, but I have never heard a band truly pull off covering the complexity of a Dickey Betts solo. That was what I walked into. I had to shuffle all the way to the back. From there, I watched as this band just nailed song after song. The star of the show was the lead guitar.

Guy looked to be pretty young. I was sending Sunny all-caps text messages every ten seconds.

GET OVER HERE
ROBERTS
HURRY
BEST BAND
WHERE ARE YOU

Fifteen minutes later, I saw him come in the front door. He spotted me waving to him. Just as he managed to get to me after wiggling his way through the packed crowd, the band said they had time for only one more. Sunny was miffed at this, but he was sure glad he made it once he heard that last song. After, the band came out into the crowd and mingled. I approached the lead guitar. I had to know how old this kid was. But there was no way I could get to him. All the prettiest girls in there just swarmed him. God was I envious. This kid had the right stuff. The bass player walked by as I tried to find a window to talk to him.

I shouted: "How old's the kid, anyway?"

"Who, Jonny?"

"Yeah, Jonny."

"Eighteen."

Eighteen! I couldn't believe it. To be eighteen and to be absolutely shredding like that, to me it was unfathomable. The only way I could think to rationalize it was to assume that was all he did. Just play the damn guitar all day, every day. For years. Talent takes you only so far. Perspiration gets people places. This kid had clearly been payin' his dues. I don't know how else to explain to myself how someone that young could be that good. Sunny found me and said we had to go.

"Where to?"

"Tootsie's."

"Tootsie's?"

"Tootsie's."

"How'd you hear of that place?"

"Guy up on the rooftop said we had to go there. It's THE place."

"Yeah, better n' here?"

"Well, there's no more music."

"True. Okay, let's go.

"Jonny's got all the girls anyway."

In Tootsie's, we found Broadway's Mecca. Like all the other Broadway bars that night, it was packed with people. As soon as we got in there, a cute young woman grabbed Sunny by the hand and led him and, by default, me, up to Tootsie's top floor. Up there, of course, live music. The band was yelling out to the crowd in between each song. The lead singer said for twenty bucks, they'd play any song requested. I was incredulous. But I wasn't going to be that guy who requests something obscure like Ry Cooder. Instead, I watched to see what kind of material the crowd wanted. Garth Brooks was requested by a friend of Sunny's new friend. This friend was young and very cute as well. She winked at me. She looked over to her friend two-stepping with Sunny. She said she had friends in low places. Hence the song. I liked her immediately.

We went to the area in front of the stage. I did my best to show her my stuff. I didn't believe him at the time, but my gym teacher in the eighth grade told us lads that an effective two stepper is catnip. Hook, line and sinker, he said. He had a module in eighth grade gym where he taught basic footwork, twirls and flips and so on. My crush back then whispered in my ear that he was right. My crush knew how to motivate me. I went above and beyond trying to master the art of dancing to songs about pick-up trucks, lost love, and dusty back roads. In several of the small towns I've lived in across the west, this gym lesson has proved the most useful skill I think I ever learned from my entire education, including expensive Dartmouth. In fact, the girl who I am dating now, it's how we met.

I returned to Taos a little while back after living up in Red Lodge. In Red Lodge, my two-stepping skills were polished at the Bull n' Bear Saloon. At the time of Run For Roses we were on a short break because she said she wanted to focus solely on getting her cosmetics certificate for a better job in Taos. When I returned to my job at the local paper after this trip with Sunny, she would be all certified and ready to earn, save, buy a house and settle down. She has her life planned out. Mine too. I like her a lot, but I find myself chafing under her determinism. She's only twenty-two and has each minute of each day planned. There were times when she lets loose, but they were rare. When those times came, like the night I met her dancing, she's simply irresistible. I fell hard.

Sunny was in a different boat with his girl. They'd been together since high school and were now living in the town of Okotoks. Okotoks is near enough for her to commute to Calgary and near enough for Sunny to go work the family ranch near Longview. He manages the whole thing now, his dad handing over the reigns a few years ago. They too were on a break because she wanted urban. She's an accountant at an oil and gas company that drills for oil in South America. Frequently she's in Colombia for business. She likes the Calgary to Bogota lifestyle. Sunny likes the ranching life. As I mentioned earlier, Sunny and I made a pact that we would be open to flirting but nothing more on the trip. It would just complicate to go any further. We respect the women in our lives. But by the same token, we were both open to maximizing the degree to which we flirted. Insofar as we thought possible. So, Sunny was on the dance floor and so was I. I was trying to show my stuff, but there were so many damn people, I was stifled. My dancing partner nonetheless was surprised at what I was capable of in the tight space.

I don't know why, but I told her that Sunny and I were from New Orleans. I did a poor job of trying to say it with a thick New Orleanian accent. Tara said she and her friend Jocelyn and a few others were in town for the hockey game. They were visiting from Cincinnati one of the friends was getting married soon. Bach party. I'd never met anyone from Cincinnati. I didn't know there were hockey fans in that town. She said that they weren't really the biggest fans but knew that a playoff hockey game in Nashville would be worth it. Anyway, we danced. After Garth Brooks, I gave the singer a twenty.

"Whaddaya want?"

"Something from Nawlins!"

"From where?"

"Nawlins!"

"From what?

"NAWLINS!"

Tara: "He's from New Orleans and wants you to play something from there!"

"You're from New Orleans? So am I!"

"Play some Nawlins!"

They played Dr. John! I couldn't believe it. I had to transition from a two-step to something like a foxtrot. The crowd wasn't quite sure what they were listening to. It's fun, danceable music though, so it worked. The next request was Shania Twain and back to the two-step we went. I tried to see where Sunny was, but I'd lost him. Tara did the same with Jocelyn and, seeing she wasn't on the dance floor anymore, said to me she had to go find her friends. I felt an urge to follow her, but I let her go. I wanted to dance. Nothing else mattered.

Must've been close to last call when, with sweat dripping down my face, I felt someone's hand come down on my shoulder. Sunny had returned. I didn't even bother asking where he'd been. He said it was time for us to go.

It was time for food. At the mention of food, we were out of there in less than ten.

"Where were ya?" I said to him, far too loud on the street. In my mind, I was still on the top floor of Tootsie's.

"That girl I was dancing with took me to a different bar!"

"Really? You weren't in there that whole time?"

"No, I thought you knew we'd left?"

"I had no idea. I danced the night away. Lost a gallon of water. I need food, drink."

"Jocelyn and them are over at a food truck right now, come let's go."

"What food?"

"Hot chicken!"

"Yes, please."

"Knew you'd be into that."

"But just hang on a minute. What's been going on with Jocelyn?"

"What do you mean?"

"I mean, you remember our little pact, don't you?"

"What, about only flirting?"

"Yeah, that one."

"Oh relax, we're only havin' some fun."

"Yeah?"

"Yeah."

"Okay then, lead the way."

The next morning was difficult. It was Cyrus that woke us at six in the morning. He was going for a run. Sunny and I got in at around four in the morning. Perhaps this was Cyrus getting back at us for our undoubtedly loud entrance only two hours prior. He slammed the door on the way out. Once I'm up, I'm up. It's a reluctant reality I live with. Sunny returned to the land of nod like nothing happened. Whenever he drinks, he snores. So, he was back to snoring. I had to get out of the room. I thought about trying to catch up to Cyrus, but I just couldn't force myself. I'd find time to run in Louisville.

The thought of Louisville instantly bolted me awake. Today was the day we planned to arrive. It was Friday, May 4th. The Derby was a day away. It felt like we'd been on the road for weeks. It also felt like yesterday Sunny and I were on Frenchman Street. For a second, I panicked over whether we had our ducks in a row. Hotels, tickets, clothes, a game plan. I ran through a mental checklist. I'd found a hotel. Check. Sunny purchased our tickets, which included races that night. Check. Clothes were all that remained. We needed our Derby outfits. Couldn't go otherwise.

I went for an early morning walk to kill time. And, I was curious about what Broadway looked like at this hour in the morning. Nashville at six in the morning on a Friday is a curious place. You see a different side. You see the city slowly wake, the engine of commerce start to rumble. There is much more to Nashville than late nights, bars, and country music. I went over to Broadway first before navel-gazing on the banks of the Cumberland. Broadway was dead except for the odd drunk, the odd staff sweeping their portion of the sidewalk. The Cumberland was tonic. I walked for a ways before finding a cappuccino stand on the banks of the old river. I found a bench to watch the sunrise. I sat there for quite some time. Despite the coffee, I even managed to nod off. I woke up after falling off the thing, spilling the remains of the drink over my white shirt.

"You're going to need a napkin," said a familiar voice. Decker was sitting at the other end of the bench. He was wearing the same outfit as when I last saw him in Atlanta. He was looking straight across the river and didn't for one moment break his steely gaze. The bright morning sun was shining directly in his eyes.

"Should I be surprised that you found me again?"

"You're going to need a napkin."

148 · James Rose

"You like repeating yourself, don't you." I propped myself back up on the bench. There was a wind from the north rippling the Cumberland's surface. It was a sharp wind and I shivered as I zipped up my jacket. Decker was perfectly still.

"My business partner and I need help, are you..."

"Interested? I thought we went over this."

"My business partner..."

"Listen, we went to that address, there was nothing. You're outta your mind." I was looking right at him. I felt no urge to leave because I was so curious to hear what would next come out of this wack job's mouth. He said nothing. I looked to where he was looking and there was a long silence eventually broken by the cappuccino guy. He asked if I'd like another.

"We'll take two," Decker said.

"We found out more about you, you know."

"Good."

"My bet is you're gonna lose your shirt on that case, you keep fighting it."

"What makes you say that Meko?"

"How the hell you gonna manage to prove the horse didn't have the drugs in him."

"My business partner and I need help. Are you interested?"

"You're insane, you know that? What in God's name can Sunny and I do anyway to help you and your goddamn business partner out?"

"We need you to place a bet." For the first time, he turned to look at me. His eyes were as cold as ice. Was it his gaze or the gust of wind that sent another shiver down my spine.

"A bet?"

"A bet."

"That's it?"

"Yes."

"How come you couldn't just ask me that back in Atlanta?"

"I had to see if you would follow through."

"You had to what? What do you mean?"

"I had to see if you and Sunny would follow through."

"You mean that's why you sent us to Rowan Oak? Just to see if we would?"

"Yes."

"Really? What about that signed guestbook? What was that about?"

"Just thought it'd be a nice touch. No?"

"How'd it get there?"

"Paid some kid to break in and leave a book there with my signature."

"You mean, that whole thing was just to see if Sunny and I would do as you said?"

"Yes."

"Okay, what about the Peabody. Who was the guy threw me the Waffle House?

"Waffle House?"

"Oh please, you know who I'm talking about. You mean to say you didn't send that guy looking for us in Memphis?"

"Why would I do that?"

"Chrissake, I don't know! Why would anyone send anyone to the house William Faulkner used to live in for no apparent reason?"

"Nice house though, don't you think? Anyway, back to my earlier question, would you be willing to help my business partner and I out by placing a bet?"

"Can I know anymore before I give you an answer?"

"No."

"How about, can I know more about Zen Master?"

"Zen Master won that race fair and square."

"Okay..."

"No one believes it because no one can believe our racing program philosophy."

"And why is that?"

"Because we came from nowhere to produce a horse that dominated a race. And we have more horses where Zen Master came from. The funny thing is that our program is squeaky clean and is heads and shoulders above all the others that are completely dirty."

"Dirty how?"

"Doping."

"It's that bad?"

"Yes. It's like cycling was twenty years ago. But worse. And probably still to this day, you ask me. Where there's a will, people will cheat. Cycling, horse racing, doesn't matter. Thoroughbred racing is as dirty as they come. It's ugly. And there are billionaires with all the power in the world that want to keep it that way." Decker paused for a moment. "But I say no."

"This is hard to believe. You know that, right? What do you do differently?"

"That's a topic for another time. I have to go now, Meko. I need to know if you can place a bet for us..."

What did I have to lose by saying no? I had no clue. To me, there was nothing. Decker's proposal seemed so innocent and straightforward. To him, I said: "Okay, I'm in."

"How about Sunny."

"What do toy mean?"

"I need to know if Sunny's onboard too."

"Okay, yes we're both in."

"You can speak for him?"

"Yes."

"Good. Now, you need to do nothing more than wait for the signal to come. You understand?"

"What kind of signal are you talking about?"

"You'll know. Trust me."

"Remind me again why I want to do this?"

"You and Sunny come through for us, the money part of taking care of your sick friend...it will be taken care of. Of course, I can't cure what ails him. But sometimes money can." Decker looked over at me after he was finished talking. He smiled. Tipped his hat, stood up, brushed his overcoat and walked his way down the banks of the Cumberland River. Where he was going, I have no clue. If this guy even existed, I was beginning to wonder. Was he an apparition? Was he a figment of my own imagination?

Sunny was up and ready to go upon my return to the hostel. He had our breakfast plans worked out. Jocelyn had told him that the place to go was in Germantown and that if we didn't get there before a specific time, there was no hope. That time was rapidly approaching as I walked through the hostel's front doors. Exasperated, Sunny wanted to know where I'd been. Out for a walk, I told him. Nothing more. Telling him about my meeting by the river could wait. In Nashville's Germantown, there is Monell's. At Monell's, you feast on plates of Southern classics and comfort foods, piled high on serving plates and shared family-style with those seated at your table.

Sunny and I had no idea what to expect. We went on Jocelyn's word. Sunny was clearly smitten. But before I could ask about her, he beat me to it.

"Nothing happened. It was fun, she's great. That's it, okay?"

"Okay. They coming?"

"Dunno. Doubt it. They kept going last night after I told them we had to go. They had no intention of slowing down. Those girls could party."

"I can't even remember what we ate at that food truck.

"Hot chicken."

"Well no wonder I'm not thinking about food right now. You even hungry?"

"Meko, what I've come to learn on this trip is that when you do a road trip through the South, you don't wait until you're hungry. You just eat. We don't get food like what we've been gorging on the past week where I am. You know that."

At first, we didn't know if we were at the right place. We pulled up to an old brick house with a porch and a big family dressed to the nines in the front yard posing for a family portrait. But then Sunny saw the restaurant's sign and in we went. Inside, there was a huge table. The maitre d' asked if we had reservations. Sunny said we didn't. She wondered if there was only the two of us. We nodded yes. We were in luck. There happened to be two spots left open at the table. The first course was minutes from being served. The maitre d' sat us and everyone at the table stared. Everyone was well dressed, had serviette's over their laps. Sunny and I absolutely looked like we'd spent the night out on Broadway. The coffee stain on my white pants didn't help. I'd never been to a family-style restaurant before. The way it works: you sit at one table and the restaurant staff brings out plates of food. It's exactly as if you were at grandma's for thanksgiving. Monell's has bottled that experience among strangers.

Soon, plate after plate of incredible food emerged from the kitchen. Sunny and I had no idea this was what we'd stumbled into. We ate and ate and ate that morning. Skillet fried chicken, green beans, cheese grits, cornbread, biscuits and gravy, pork chops, pot roast, bacon, eggs, toast, smoked sausage, country ham, fried apples, pancakes, hash browns, corn pudding, and gallons of orange juice and coffee. And you had to pass bowls to the left. Monell's is proper that way. But it also makes sense when there's plate after plate coming your way and fifteen people to share it with. No one left the table hungry. It was a true feast. To my right sat Wim, the county judge. He was immaculately dressed and well mannered and had a great big belly laugh to match his appetite. To my left sat Chloe, the ultra-marathoner pharmaceutical executive. Chloe and Wim ate about the same amount of food. An astounding amount.

Sunny was seated across the table. We took the two odd seats that remained and were left to make new friends. Wim could tell I had no idea what was happening. He asked where I was from. I told him northern New Mexico. He said he'd never met someone from that part of the country and that in the South, there was an old saying: "There are no such things as strangers, only friends we haven't met yet." I laughed and tried not rolling my eyes. "It's true," he said as he passed the fried chicken.

"What brings you to Nashville?"

"My cousin and I, he's seated across the table, we're just passing through on our way to the Derby."

"Oh, is that soon?"

"Yes, tomorrow."

"From where are you passing? All the way from New Mexico?"

"No, we were in New Orleans and decided to drive north from there last weekend."

"You mean to say that you decided on driving north to Louisville from New Orleans?"

"We didn't have that planned, you're right. What happened was we got a call late at night. We were in New Orleans for the Jazz Fest, and it was Sunny's mom calling to tell that a close family friend had been diagnosed with late-stage cancer."

"Well, I am sorry to hear that Meko. But I hope you don't mind me asking, how does the Derby fit?"

"Well, we know that this friend of ours is having financial difficulty, and—"

"You mean to say you're going to try and win money to pay medical bills at the Derby?"

"I know, it's crazy, but when we considered it, we thought, why not? See, he's got a colourful history with the Derby too. He won big back in the '80s and bought a sailboat with the money. He had to sell that boat recently to help pay for this experimental treatment that didn't end up working."

"How much did he spend?"

"To be honest, I don't know. I don't really want to know either. But he means a tonne to Sunny and me and our family and we just want to do anything we can to help him get through this. Basically, we dedicated this trip from Louisiana all the way to Derby."

"What's his name?"

"Von Rotz."

"Von what?"

"Rotz."

"Dutch, like me."

"Have you gone to the Derby before?"

"Oh yes, many times. I've made some money, lost some money. Lost more than I've made, I can tell you that."

"That right? You know the horses?"

"Not so much this year. I do know Justify is the overwhelming favourite. Anyone to not bet on him is a fool. But you never know. That's the beauty of the Derby."

Chloe, who'd been rather quiet this whole time, at the mention of Justify, chimed in.

She said, "You know there's rumours those horses aren't clean, right?"

"So I've heard."

Wim: "It's nonsense. People have been saying that for years, not knowing the extent to which they test."

Chloe: "There was a big piece in the New York Times about it just the other day."

"What the Times prints doesn't equate to truth."

"Wim, I happen to be aware of a court case that involves doping in horse racing. I wonder if you've heard of it?"

"You must be referring to the Tassajara case."

"You know about it?"

"I know that Tassajara has no chance."

"In what way?"

"They have a weak case. The interests against them are massive. Public opinion is against them. It's a fool's errand you ask me."

Chloe: "What's that case about?"

"There was a horse that won a race and one of the bettors lost big. So he sued the owner of the horse after supposed tests showed positive performance enhancers."

Wim: "And the guy is trying to prove that those tests were planted. It's lunacy! Anyway, Meko if you want my advice on betting, it's this: Don't listen to anyone. Read the numbers, analyze the odds, and then spread your bets out. It's the only way. Trust me."

"All due respect, you said you've lost more money than you've earned..."

"I have, but compared to other people who thought they had a winning tip, I've done much, much better."

JANUARY 23, 2019

Dear Lula Mae,

It's been over two months since I last wrote you. I wanted to leave my letter writing for life on the road. Meko and I are back on the road. I write this to you from Aspen, Colorado. We arrived here from Utah earlier this week. Meko wanted to catch a film at Sundance, having never before been to that extravaganza. Before Park City, we spent a weekend in Tahoe. And before Tahoe, of course, San Francisco. Two months and change in San Francisco brought mixed feelings. There's lots to get excited about in that town, but there is also plenty of frustration. It has to do with the exorbitant number of people that live there, and the high cost of everything. Excluding Eddie's, nothing is cheap in San Francisco. It's tiresome.

Now, I don't want to give the impression that I'm sour on that town. I do love it. And I love nearby Marin County and Berkeley over the Bay Bridge. I love that it's about three hours to the Sierra Nevada. I love a lot about San Francisco. But maybe it's better suited to visit than to live. Visitors and residents to a place have different sets of experience. That's easy to say in hindsight. Though isn't it true that you have to first live through a maxim to truly appreciate the simplicity?

I don't think we'll be in Aspen long. The X Games nightmare is soon upon this town and Meko wants out before the tourists arrive. We had enough of that in Park City. And what is the X Games anyway? To me, it's an entirely made for TV spectacle for the masses. Instead, give me a world cup downhill to watch down Aztec, a steep run on Ajax. We are in Aspen because Meko's here to visit an old college friend. Jack Badenhausen invited us to come stay at his place in town and ski Ajax. Meko said he was surprised when Jack asked whether he'd like to join his staff as a writer for the newspaper. Jack's the assistant editor. His boss' name is Norman. It's called the Aspen Herald and Jack told Meko, who told me that the paper is looking for someone who doesn't mind shit pay and tight deadlines. Meko was taken aback. He had no expectations Jack would make such an offer.

Meko wasn't sure if he'd accept. He said he needed time on the road to consider. I think the plan is for us to drive south next to Arroyo Seco. Sunny wrote to tell that he didn't mind Meko keeping me as a companion if it meant helping him deal with girl troubles back home. Apparently Sunny is doing quite fine at the moment. Maybe you can fill me in? Anyway, I suppose that's my purpose, to be of comfort and conciliation for lovesick Meko. I don't mind. There's a life of adventure that comes with that role. The girl he was hanging around with in San Francisco evidently didn't work out. Meko said he wasn't into the key-bump-cocaine set. The one back in Taos, I think they are talking again. They FaceTimed for three hours on Christmas Day. And not just as friends, but more so. I think Meko realized that she may be the girl for him. But he's not sure. He never is. He says that in that department, he doesn't want to settle. I looked at him when he said that. He thought I took it the wrong way. He clarified by saying that by settle, he meant he didn't want to convince himself that someone was the one for him, even though that someone is worthy of his utmost respect and admiration. Some people just don't click.

I'll tell you more about all that happened in San Francisco when I next see you. I think I'll be back to Canada in February or March. Maybe it won't be until summer, I don't know. I don't like the idea of living in the New Mexico heat through the summer. I think Meko is aware of this. The one important point I want to mention is that we did, in fact, go down to Monterey for a visit. Monterey is beautiful. Nearby Carmel, even nicer. I don't know why we ended up going there. All Meko would say was that he had to go down there, specifically Carmel, for work. He had a "real humdinger" of a story he was reporting on (his words). As we know, his work is journalism. I don't know what exactly was in Carmel. We stayed at a motel and spent a couple days on someone's ranch. Beautiful horses ran around in the adjacent ranchlands. I'm talking horse racing calibre. There is probably a connection between Decker he has spoken about in his Run For Roses story. But he never said to me that was who we were visiting. Not once.

I wasn't allowed to set foot in the ranch house. I just sat there on the big porch with this big ol' black lab and we seemed to get along just fine. We had a deep conversation. Here's a little summary:

I asked him, "Do you often think about dying?"

"Yes, these are subjects that we think about all the time but don't necessarily talk about. Everybody has thought about if they want to be cremated, buried, or whatever."

"What's your preference?"

"I want a big 25-foot pink statue that holds my grave. Or I also might like the way the Indians did it. They hang you up on the top of a tree and the birds eat you. No, really I would probably choose cremating."

"Are there any positive aspects of aging?"

"Plenty. You are more thoughtful because you don't act as quickly anymore. When I turned fourteen it was the first time I felt young for my age. Ten dropped on me like a tonne of bricks – there is something about that number – but when fourteen came along I felt good about it."

"What made you feel younger?"

"I don't know. I mean why relate to a number anyway? I used to be very quick. I would be able to leave the room and be back before you noticed. When you can't do that anymore you need to change the style of how you do things. But I'm very interested in life and you don't want to lose that."

Maybe the most prescient thing he said was to just stay in the moment. In the now. Like if you're not cold, hungry, wet, tired, sick, then you're doing okay. Anyway, let's just assume that Meko was doing interviews. Maybe he'll fill me in on our way from Colorado back to Taos. Hope so. I would also like to write a bit about what has happened since we left the Bay Area. On our way out from San Francisco, we first arrived to South Lake Tahoe for a ski weekend and celebrated a friend of Meko's birthday. A big group of us rented a huge Bavarian-style ski chalet near Heavenly. While they all skied and nursed hangovers, I was left to hold the fort.

Meko did take me each of the three mornings for runs up the Heavenly slope before the ski lifts started spinning. He has the kind of ski equipment that allows for walking uphill and then skiing down with a fixed heel. So as he walked up the slope, I ran around the freshly groomed ski run and then I tried my level best not to have a heart attack by trying to keep up with him on the way down. Heavenly in the middle of January isn't exactly my idea of heaven, but it sure is comfortable weather. It's the middle of winter there and you'd think it's March in the Rockies. Blue skies, temperatures just below zero and of course, plenty of sunshine. From Tahoe, we did a straight shot across Nevada to Utah. The Nevada countryside is desolate. There's a beauty in that. You drive through places like Golconda and Battle Mountain and you're thinking this is another planet compared to the west slope of the Sierra Nevada.

Upon our arrival to Park City, Meko was entrenched in ski mode. He wanted to not just check out Sundance the film festival, but also the Sundance ski resort. But the skiing he really wanted was at Alta. Up Little Cottonwood Canyon, Alta is one of only two ski resorts in North America where it's still skiing only, no snowboarding. Meko had to go there. Unfortunately, the snow wasn't very good on the days he skied. To have a great day of skiing, he says you need to find balance between terrain, snow, and scenery. Alta has terrain and scenery and usually the snow. Not that time, oh well. We walked around Park City while Sundance was in full swing. Plenty of LA stilettos trying to walk up the sloped (and iced) main street. More than a handful of the retailers in Park City just leave town while the festival is on. They rent their space out to production companies, camera makers, basically any industry player in American cinema that wants to showcase their wares and throw a party.

Meko couldn't believe the eclectic nature of all who was there. He said he wound up at a party hosted by Canon, where he met an independent director trying to sell his feature film. The director said he financed the project with credit card debt without any guarantee of a buyer. Later that night, Meko went to a fancy whisky bar and encountered a whole other Park City subset: the wealthy social conservative. Until that night at the bar, Meko said he'd never met someone who believed that since God put oil and gas underneath the Earth's crust, then for that reason alone, it was justifiable for man to drill for it and burn it. To this wealthy individual, it was God's plan all along for man to burn hydrocarbons. All kinds of different people in that town. And no, we never did see Redford.

And here we now are in Aspen. Meko's been skiing every day we've been here. I don't know if he has much else to do. Who knows where he's at with his work. He is pretty excited about trying out fiction for the first time. He said that he never knew how much energy he had to pour into that form of storytelling. Giving himself permission, believing that he could do it, he said he felt revitalized by it all. Teddy Roosevelt once said, believe and you're halfway there. Well said, Ted. In Aspen, Meko says the skiing here is much better than expected. Many people think of this place as glitz and nothing more. The skiing is actually remarkable. We've been lucky to get plenty of fresh snow. Meko has taken me out a few early mornings and I can vouch for the quality and quantity of snow.

Now, I'm sure you're curious to know what next happened in Run For Roses. I felt the exact same way as I waited and waited until we hit the road again. Two whole months I waited. Not that I lost sleep over it. Still, if for no other reason to find out what happened with deathly ill Von Rotz. Well, you're in luck. I can tell you in this letter all that happened between Nashville and Louisville. Yes, below you will hopefully get closure on a few details that I am sure have been driving you mad since my last note. Although he did wrap up the tale, he left one more carrot dangling. The last bit was for our return drive to Taos. He said I could think of it like the story's epilogue. So, I'll have to wait until we make the final push south before I can write that part of the story. In the meantime, here's my attempt at retelling a story told to me sitting shotgun in a beat up truck from San Francisco all the way to Aspen, Colorado.

Xoxox
Foxworth

* * *

How Meko and Sunny were shown true Southern Hospitality at the Kentucky Derby by local beauty Scarlet O'Hara. How they ended up betting their ten grand.

Sunny drove us north out of Nashville. We blasted out of that town with a singular focus set upon our final destination. That focus was soon interrupted by caves. In southern Kentucky, a half-hour drive northeast of Bowling Green is Mammoth Cave National Park. Neither of us had heard of the place. And had we not stopped for gas in beautiful Bowling Green, I don't think we would've paid a visit. Inside the gas station, there was blown up photo after photo of the caves. The clerk was passionate about them.

"Best caves in the world," he said as he took my credit card.

"Yeah?"

"Best caves in the damn world." He stared at me and like he was about to start welling up.

To Sunny in the car, I said: "We gotta check out these caves."

"Come again?"

"Caves. Best in the world, I'm told."

"There's caves around here?"

"Yeah, just up the road. Guy in there said to check them out. Find yourself. Experience them in all their wonderful glory. And when you go, say hi to Billy for me."

Sunny said, "We go to those caves, we can walk around in them?"

"Yeah. Wouldn't be a bad idea. I don't know about you but I feel horrible."

"Last night and this morning, I'm feeling it too."

"Let's check out some caves. What else we gotta do? We'll get to Louisville and then?"

"Gotta get the clothes."

"True. And where's our hotel?"

"Closest, cheapest I could find still available was a Super 8 in La Grange."

"Where's that?"

"About an hour east of Churchill Downs. Might be smarter to just end up there after a day doing what we gotta do in Louisville."

At the Mammoth Caves, Sunny and I arrived to a deserted national park, grey skies, sharp winds, speckles of rain. That part of Kentucky is densely forested. There was nothing much to see above ground. We walked over to Mammoth Cave itself, fighting wind and the enormous amount of food in our stomachs. Inside the cave itself, the park's most well known, it was much more comfortable than being in the elements. There must've been some sort of weather inversion. The inside was warm and humid. After walking for about five minutes, Sunny said he needed to sit down. He wasn't feeling well. I went ahead and after a while, I noticed there wasn't a peep from behind. I called Sunny's name, no answer. I turned around and walked back to where I left him. Sunny was strewn across Mammoth Cave's rocky floor. Out like a light. Fast asleep, completely dead to the world. Who but Sunny could fall asleep in a place like this? But then I yawned. So, I sat down beside him. He'd be up in no time and we'd continue exploring the best caves in the world. I yawned again. And then, I too was out for the count.

"Meko, get up," Sunny said, as he shook me awake. I hadn't had that deep of a nap in years.

"What time is it?"

"Three-thirty."

"Three-thirty?"

"Yeah, we slept in this cave for the past two hours."

"Holy shit, you serious?" He showed me his watch to confirm that yes, we'd napped in Mammoth Cave for the two whole hours.

To Sunny I said, "How you feel?"

"Unbelievable. You?"

"Same."

"Come on, let's go. There's horse racing tonight we can still catch."

"There is?"

"Yeah, they do a different set of races today and then the big Derby is to-morrow. I looked it up while you were asleep."

"How long you been up?"

"Twenty minutes or so. You weren't waking when I tried earlier."

Outside the cave, someone was walking over to us. Sunny said he was staff at the nearby River Styx campground.

"You get him awake?" He said to Sunny.

"Thanks Bill, yeah, here he is."

"You guys aren't the first to sleep in there, I'll tell ya that."

"Really?"

"Aw hell, you kiddin'? Most times it's bums or kids gettin' shitfaced. You guys don't like either, so now I can say...well I'm not sure what I can say."

"Didn't think it'd be so sleepy."

"That's a rare phenomenon you don't see every day. Usually it's drafty in there. Here have some o' this...it'll help ya wake up. You're goin' to the Derby." Bill handed Sunny a glass bottle.

"What's this Bill?"

"Bit a Kentucky hooch won't hurt ya. Pa made that."

"Bit a shine for us?"

"Well, you asked what I was drinkin' earlier. How else you think I get through days like this. Only people in this whole damn park are couple guys nappin' with Florida plates. Now, Sunny, you remember what I told you right? And don't forget, you don't wanna waste your time on that expensive shit they sell at the track. This'll do ya right. Anyway, ya'll take care now, ya hear? Sunny, good meetin' ya." Bill handed the bottle to Sunny and returned back to his office.

Sunny handed me the bottle. I looked at him like he was crazy. "Nope. Not right now. Not after that sleep."

"Okay, fine. Later."

"How bout we try something new today. We stay sober and save it all up for tomorrow."

"You think we can do that?"

"We can try."

"Even if we go to the Oaks tonight?"

"Trust me, it'll make tomorrow that much better."

"You know we gotta figure a few things out for tomorrow, right?

"Like with the bets and everything?"

"If we don't have our game plan set before we start throwin' a few back, especially with whatever the hell is in this bottle, we may be in trouble."

"Then let's use the Oaks for reconnaissance. Remind me again what the Oaks race is?"

"Come on, let's go. I'll tell ya in the car. Bill helped me out with it too. Gave me some betting tips."

We made it to the twin spires of Churchill Downs by six o'clock. Of course, every city is different, but I'd never been to a place quite like Louisville. In Louisville, we found a midsize American city. It's not far enough south to be considered southern. Nor is it far enough north to be true blue yankee. The Ohio River runs through the heart of the city. Cross the river to the north and you're in Indiana. Louisville is also too far south to be considered part of the rust belt. That doesn't mean it's not industrial. Kentucky's coal industry is headquartered there and on a grey spring day such as how it was upon our virgin arrival, Louisville looked industrial. The neighbourhoods we drove through to get to Churchill Downs all had patchy roads, white clapboard houses, weedy front lawns, and plenty of stars and stripes. Churchill Downs is in the south part of town. To get to the commercial core, it's a good twenty minutes through traffic. Sunny and I thought we'd go downtown for a bite to eat after. Yes, we were already thinking about eating by the time we got to Churchill Downs.

There were still a few races left, but the majority of them had taken place. The tickets I bought included entry to the Oaks, a gender-specific race allowing only 3-year-old female horses, or fillies, to qualify and compete. The Derby is open to eligible colts, geldings or fillies. The only other difference is, the Oaks is 1 1/8 miles long, while the Derby is extended a furlong at 1 1/4 miles. Our tickets were infield tickets. The only ones we could afford. So, into the infield we went. We walked by statue after statue of horses and jockeys and dead civic leaders. Hard to fathom that this was the 144th year of this annual event.

"You notice everyone's wearin' pink?" I said to Sunny.

"Tradition. They decorate the track in pink bunting and everyone's asked to add pink to their wardrobe. It's for raising cash toward cancer."

"You got any pink?"

"Nope. You?"

"When we gonna go shop?"

"How bout we go tomorrow morning first thing at a mall. We're not wearin' pink but we can still donate over here." Sunny pointed to a bin.

"And I guess over at those wooden booths is where we make the bets."

"Yeah, something like that. Why don't we go over there and try one."

I found a booth with a well dressed older gent in a pink tie. He could tell right away that this was my first time here. I told him I'd like to make a bet. He said, "And how would you like to bet?" Before answering, I asked him to explain the basics. He was great. I'll sum up what he told me here. The most common bets you can make are the basic bets: Win, Place, Show. These wagers usually offer the lowest risk and are recommended to rookies like Sunny and me. The next level up, just outside of regular basic bets, would be your exotic bets: placing a wager on more than one outcome whether it is betting on more than one race or betting on the consecutive finishers in a single race.

A Win bet is the easiest bet you can make. You simply pick the horse you think will cross the finish line first. A Place bet is betting on a horse that you think will finish in first or second. If the horse you bet on finishes in one of the two top spots, you collect the amount shown in the place column. This bet is less risky than a Win bet, but also offers a smaller return. A Show bet is a wager on a horse to finish within the top three positions. If the horse shows (finishes first, second or third), this is a winning bet. The payout is exactly the same, even if the horse finishes first or second. To "bet across the board" is to place a bet that is a combination of Win, Place, and Show wagers. If you bet a horse across the board, you are betting them to

Win, Place, and Show. If the horse wins the race, then you collect the pay-outs displayed on all three bets. An Exacta bet is successfully predicting the winning horse and the second-place finisher in that exact order. A Trifecta bet is similar to an Exacta wager, except you are betting which horses you think will finish in the top three positions in that race in that order. With a Superfecta bet, you are selecting the top four finishers in order. This is the hardest of the single-race exotics and yields the highest payouts.

The first bet I placed was for a horse named Horatius to win outright. Sunny meanwhile wanted to try his luck betting across the board on Streamline Promenade. I'm not sure about Sunny, but I was nervous about making my bet. I had this feeling like I was being sold snake oil. I was fork-ing over ten hard earned bucks for something I knew absolutely nothing about. I suppose you could say that the thrill of watching the race can only come with an admission price. And I'm not talking admission to Churchill Downs, but admission to the sport of betting. You gotta pay to play. We both lost. Horatius came seventh, and Streamline Promenade was disquali-fied for interfering with another horse. It was a learning lesson for us. De-spite the odds placed on horses, anything can happen. Despite the best laid plans, life can happen. Sunny and I didn't stay long. Stone cold sober among drunken horse gamblers, it was time we leave to see downtown Louisville.

Louisville is peculiar. From these streets come all kinds of people. Cas-sius Clay, Jim James, T. Coleman du Pont, St. Elmo Brody, Harold Poole, and many more. The Louisville Slugger, I can't forget the Louisville Slug-ger. There's a museum in Louisville dedicated to nothing but the ol' Slug-ger. As there should be. There is nothing sweeter than cracking a clean homer off the end of a Slugger. The sound, the feel, there's magic in those finely crafted pieces of wood. I would be remiss to not mention the Ken-tucky bourbon industry. The big boys like Woodford Reserve, Jim Beam all have a presence in the city. The corn mash in which they procure those alcoholic vapours may exist out in the country, but there they all are in Louisville. Tasting rooms are everywhere.

Sunny saw the look in my eye upon seeing the confusion of bourbon tasting rooms. He tapped me on the shoulder as we walked down Market Street. I looked over. He was showing me in his jacket breast pocket Ol' Billy Boy's finest. He said to me, "Now don't you get any ideas. We got ourselves some o' that real fine moonshine." We went for food at a bar on the corner of Main and Market. Everyone in there was in full Derby attire. The party had started. This, however, was a classier joint. The oak-paneled door, the leather seats, the lowly lit interior, this was old money steakhouse territory.

We sat at the bar. A group of young women stood around a Latin looking character at the end of the bar. The bartender saw our curiosity. He told us it was just another jockey full of bourbon. He said to us in a distinct southern drawl that the Derby jockeys would have girls hanging off them within two minutes of arrival if they chose to hit the bars. And they are notorious drinkers. This one, Schiffer his name, last year broke a bottle over Morgan's head. Morgan, another jockey. It was the night after the Derby. Schiffer and his opponent both placed better than expected, but no matter. The night was for drinking. With what little they earned from their reasonable showings, they pissed it away on bourbon. Schiffer was thrown in the drunk tank that night and had his hand bandaged. His bloody fingers bandaged from broken glass.

Schiffer looked over at us. He had the bartender pour us each a couple fingers of Basil Hayden. For Sunny and I, it took all of our willpower to say no. "Tomorrow, we drink," Sunny said, dead serious. Schiffer couldn't believe what he was hearing. One of the girls started taunting us with a real sneer in her voice. Schiffer asked her to be quiet in an Argentinean accent. Eventually, he shrugged and let Sunny and I mind our own business of ordering a couple rib-eyes. The cranberry juice in front of me was fabulous.

Sunny sipped club soda. I could see in the mirror behind the bar that Schiffer was looking at us with amazement. With envy almost.

"Amigos," he finally said.

"Thanks for the bourbon, but not tonight."

"Self-control," he said with narrowed eyes. "I admire."

"You're racing tomorrow?" Sunny asked.

"Amigo..."

"Yes?"

"Ven aca."

"I don't speak Spanish."

"Momento," I said. Growing up in northern New Mexico, you learn Spanish. I walked over to Schiffer and introduced myself.

"Meko, mi primo Sunny."

"Me llamo Raphael Gonzalez. También conocido como Schiffer."

"Schiffer?"

"Si, señor. Schiffer es el nombre del caballo que gané por primera vez."

"Nos vemos mañana?"

"Mañana corro," said Schiffer.

"Lo mejor de las suertes."

"Eres Mexicano?"

"No señor. Nuevo Mexico. Taos."

"Muy bueno. Me gustas dos." I returned to my seat and Schiffer toasted Sunny and me. He slugged his drink and then downed the two he'd ordered for us. Sunny and I ate our steaks and watched with amazement as the jockey full of bourbon swam upstream in his own whiskey river.

On his way out, Schiffer put his arms around us and dropped his head between ours. His hands were scarred and dirty. He was missing the end of his pinky from the first knuckle down. This guy was a pirate. He stood no more than 5'3". And he was positively hammered but still stringing sentences together. He first looked at Sunny in the eye for a long time. Then he turned his gaze toward me.

"Estás aquí por la razón correcta. Quiero ayudar." Seeing the look of confusion on Sunny's face, he switched to simple English.

"I want to help."

Sunny: "How so?"

"Mañana, tomorrow, look for Shey Gompa."

"Shey what?" Schiffer was gone before he could tell us anymore. Sunny and I looked at each other and burst out laughing. Our steaks held our attention. We had no time parsing the jockey full of bourbon's words.

Well into the night, we finally arrived to our La Grange Super 8. Everything in town was booked solid for the Derby. Including our Super 8. It was everything we needed. It was cheap and clean. We would not be spending much time here. When I got to the front desk, the man asked for my name.

"Torres," I said. "Meko Torres."

"One second." Took the guy ten minutes of scrolling before he looked up at me. "Sorry sir, it looks as though your name isn't in our system." My heart sank. Sunny, standing beside me, had that look in his eye.

"This can't be right. I made the booking earlier this week. I called the Super 8 in La Grange, this one right here and made my booking."

"One second sir, let me check again. Do you have your confirmation code?"

"It's on my phone but it's dead." The man behind the counter continued scrolling. Nothing was coming up.

"I'm sorry sir, but there's nothing booked here with your name. Are you sure you made the reservation?"

"Ya. I'm sure." Sunny could sense my blood pressure was rising.

"Meko, relax. He's only doing his job. Power up your phone and show the confirmation email." I handed over my phone. What felt like a lifetime passed before I could turn it on. The email with the confirmation was found. I showed it to the man behind the desk.

"That's why," he said.

"What's why? See here, I have a reservation!"

"You called the Super 8 in La Grange, Oregon."

"I what?"

"Look…" He showed me the small print at the bottom. Yep, I'd called the wrong Super 8.

"You can't be serious."

"Never seen that happen before," he said with a laugh.

"Well, is there anything you can do about it?"

"Sorry sir, we're fully booked."

Sunny looked like he was going to strangle me.

"There's absolutely nothing?"

"Real sorry sir, there's nothing."

"Well, okay then." I could barely get those words out. Sunny wouldn't look at me. What were we to do now? We had nowhere to sleep. There wasn't a room in the entire metropolitan area available.

"Well, I guess we could open up Ol' Billy Boy and sleep in the car?" I didn't know what else to say.

"I guess you're right Meko. I guess you're right."

So, that's what we did. We went back to the Focus. Reclined the two front seats and while Sunny was fishing in his bag for the hooch, I turned on some of that old McDowell. We hadn't listened to Mississippi Fred since Rowan Oak. This was a night for the blues. Sunny presented the bottle.

"You sure you wanna crack this? I think we should consider waiting for tomorrow."

"This is gonna be a long night. You ever slept in a Focus before?"

"Have you?"

"Well, no."

And then there was a knock on Sunny's window. We couldn't see who it was. It was so dark out there, I told Sunny to hide the hooch. I thought it was a cop. "Hang on. Don't say we're sleeping here. Tell him we're just gonna be on our way. We'll go out into the country or something." Sunny rolled down his window. To our surprise, it wasn't a cop. It was the man from behind the counter.

"Gentleman," he said. "You're in luck."

Our faces lit up.

"You got room for us?"

"It ain't much but yes, I found you a room."

A room had come up after the Super 8 security had to kick out the young group of guys from Staten Island who were caught smoking dope in their strictly non-smoking room. These guys had been there for the past couple of nights and caused a serious ruckus. The man behind the counter finally had a good reason to kick them out. Us.

So, that's where we ended up. In the room formerly occupied by the messiest pigs you can imagine. There was no time for the staff to clean it. We didn't care. Back in the jacket pocket went Ol' Billy. As we walked through the sliding doors of the magnificent La Grange Super 8, that rowdy pack of wolves ran past us and into the night. They had bloodshot eyes, torn t-shirts and immediately began howling at the moon shining above. They didn't seem to care one bit. I slept fine after our man behind the desk brought us clean linens. Sunny had all the windows open and sprayed his fancy Belgian cologne everywhere to mask the foul smell.

"Where'd you get that stuff anyway?"

"What, the cologne?

"Yeah, didn't know you were a cologne guy."

"Well, we are going to the Derby tomorrow."

"So what?"

"You smell good, you look good, you feel good. You feel good, you bet good. You bet good...understand?"

"Okay, Sundance. I'm gonna set the alarm for eight. We'll get up, eat and go find our wardrobe, okay?" As we rapidly approached the land of nod, Sunny spoke.

"Meko?"

"Yeah?"

"You awake?"

"Yeah." There was a pause.

"We made it."

"Yeah."

"You believe that?"

"Been quite the trip."

"Tomorrow's for Von Rotz."

"Wish he was here."

Derby Day

We woke to hard rain, out the door to Louisville by nine. Our Uber driver said we could find appropriate clothing in St. Matthews. He let us off at a mall in that tony part of the city and he promised us he wouldn't leave. Having no idea where to shop for Derby clothes, we floundered around until ending up at a Dillard's. As we shopped, we tried answering unanswered questions. Was the Derby rain or shine? Were we going to be in the pouring rain all day in the infield? How much did we need to drink to stay warm? What is appropriate to wear at the Derby? Depends on who you ask. Sure, you can wear pink suits and a pink top hat. But that's one end of the spectrum. You could go the other way and be traditional. Blacks and greys. Nice clothes are the common denominator. Jeans and runners won't work. Gotta tuck, and if there's a fedora that fits, go for it.

A costume party, nothing more. For every clownish outfit you see, and there are many, that's what Derby Day has become to a lot of people. You go to Lexington's Keeneland for a more reserved, more refined, scaled-back version of a horse race. Churchill Downs is for the masses. And the masses increasingly think of the Derby as a mint julep fuelled costume party. More on the mint julep later. Sunny and I went with pale blue blazers and white shirts. I found a cream coloured Derby branded fedora. Sunny found a pair of brown loafers. He asked me my opinion on the loafers. I said he should go for snakeskin.

"We never found about that, did we?

"About the guy who threw me the Waffle House?"

"Yeah."

"I know, who knows, maybe he'll come to our rescue we drink a little too much today."

"Wouldn't that be nice? What about that Decker dude?"

"What about him?"

"You willing to admit yet that you made him up?"

"He found me in Nashville, you know…"

"Oh, here we go again…"

"No, I'm serious! I've been meaning to tell you. He said he needed us to place a bet is all…"

"Huh?"

"He said he sent us up to Rowan Oak just to see if he would. All he needs us to do is place a bet today."

"Meko, come on."

"I'm serious. We sat on a bench on the banks of the Cumberland. It was when I went out for a walk while you were happily snoring away. Remember? Cyrus slammed the door?"

"He came back and apologized for that, you know."

"He did?"

"Yeah, he said he felt so ashamed. That he sinned. He apologized. I accepted his apology. We hugged."

"Anyway, that's all Decker wants. For us to place a bet. Trouble is, I don't know what bet to place."

"Course you don't."

"All he said was you'll know it when you see it."

"Love it. You know this guy's a figment of your own imagination, right?"

"Well we know he does exist. He was in the papers."

"Ya but that doesn't mean you're not hallucinating him. Hell, far as I was concerned, I was talking to Carrie Underwood all night in Nashville. But she said her name was Jocelyn. Beer goggles, Meko."

"Jocelyn was cute. Not a far stretch."

"Just sayin'. Anyway, let's pay up here and get goin'! It's Derby Day Meko! Derby Day!"

Dressed to kill, Sunny and I walked out of the St. Matthews Dillard's on a rainy Saturday looking for our loyal Uber driver. Ronny was still there. He looked at us in our clothes and laughed. Typical, he said. Ronny'd seen it before. Not his first time at the zoo.

"Thought you guys got lost in there. Want me to take you to Churchill Downs?"

"Thanks, Ronny. They still run the races if it's rainin', right?"

Ronny looked in the rearview with an arched eyebrow. "Where ya'll from anyway?"

"First time to Kentucky. Sunny's from Alberta up in Canada, I'm from Taos, New Mexico."

"Welcome to Louisville. How you like it here so far?"

"Got here yesterday, went to the Oaks, not a bad little town, Ronny."

"You guys party last night then?"

"No we pledged one sober night on this road trip we're on. Last night."

"No shit. No bourbon or anythin'?

"We came close, but no," Sunny said. "You think this rain's gonna let up?"

"Not a chance. Gonna get worse, I hear."

Sunny said, "Well I guess it's time we crack ol' grandad?"

"You mean the shine?"

Ronny: "I hear you guys talkin' about stump water back there?"

Sunny: "Yeah, we got ourselves some corn squeezin's."

"Pass the tanglefoot."

Sunny: "Ronny, you don't mind?

"What's that?"

"We indulge some tiger sweat in your car?"

"You gonna sip on some o' that white lightnin', you better let me have some."

"Give it here, Sunny."

"Be my guest." Sunny produced the fancy little number from his new blazer's breast pocket. It glowed.

"Must be only about ten ounces in there, I reckon." I popped the cork, looked in the bottle. Was I seeing things? In the vapours wafting in the air from out of the bottle, I saw the face of ol' Virgil Caine himself.

"You see that Sunny?" He nodded yes. Slowly, I raised Ol' Billy to my lips.

"Here's to the first o' the day, fellas."

Ronny: "To old DH Lawrence!"

"HOOOO. Some fine yak yak there!"

"All right, hand it over," Sunny said. He looked at it for a few seconds and then down the hatch.

"HOO-WEE!"

Ronny said, "All right, hand it over...HOT DAMN! Some panto piss you got there boys!"

Sunny took the glowing bottle from our driver and put it away. We needed it for the whole day and into the wee hours. Waste not, want not. Sunny saw the look in my eye, and he shook his head no.

"Contain yourself, Meko. This needs to last."

"Hey Ronny, how long till we're at the track? I'm shitfaced!"

"With this traffic, damn, lookin' at thirty to forty-five."

"Shit, we should get something else to get us going."

"You want, I can pull over at the next lights. There's a liquor store there will sell you what you need."

Ronny did just that. We asked him for a local recommendation. Something other than Woodford Reserve or Jim Beam. Ronny took less than a second to reply. "Old Fitzgerald."

And so out we walked from that sleazy liquor store on the corner of God knows where Louisville with a cute little bottle of Old Fitz.

"Here's to the second o' the day, fellas," I said as we sped off and rejoined the traffic toward the track.

Ronny was a fountain of knowledge. We lucked out having him as our driver. After Sunny asked him why the mint julep was so popular, he recited from memory a poem written by 19th-century Lexington judge and journalist Joshua Soule Smith.

The Mint Julep

Then comes the zenith of man's pleasure. Then comes the julep – the mint julep. Who has not tasted one has lived in vain. The honey of Hymettus brought no such solace to the soul; the nectar of the gods is tame beside it. It is the very dream of drinks, the vision of sweet quaffings.

The Bourbon and the mint are lovers. In the same land they live, on the same food are they fostered. The mint dips its infant leaf into the same stream that makes the Bourbon what it is. The corn grows in the level lands through which small streams meander. By the brook-side the mint grows.

As the little wavelets pass, they glide up to kiss the feet of the growing mint, and the mint bends to salute them. Gracious and kind it is, living only for the sake of others. Like a woman's heart it gives its sweetest aroma when bruised.

Among the first to greet the spring, it comes. Beside the gurgling brooks that make music in the fields, it lives and thrives. When the bluegrass be-

gins to shoot its gentle sprays to sun, mint comes, and its sweetest soul drinks at the crystal brook. It is virgin then.

But soon it must be married to old Bourbon. His great heart, his warmth of temperament, and that affinity which no one understands, demands the wedding.

How shall it be? Take from the cold spring some water, pure as angels are; mix it with sugar till it seems like oil. Then take a glass and crush your mint within it with a spoon – crush it around the borders of the glass and leave no place untouched.

Then throw the mint away – it is a sacrifice. Fill with cracked ice the glass; pour in the quantity of Bourbon which you want. It trickles slowly through the ice. Let it have time to cool, then pour your sugared water over it. No spoon is needed; no stirring allowed – just let it stand a moment. Then around the brim place sprigs of mint, so that the one who drinks may find taste and odor at one draft.

Then when it is made, sip it slowly. August suns are shining, the breath of the south wind is upon you. It is fragrant, cold and sweet – it is seductive. No maiden's kiss is tenderer or more refreshing, no maiden's touch could be more passionate.

Sip it and dream – you cannot dream amiss. Sip it and dream – it is a dream itself. No other land can give so sweet solace for your cares; no other liquor soothes you in melancholy days.

Sip it and say there is no solace for the soul, no tonic for the body like old Bourbon whiskey.

Sunny and I had tears running down our cheeks as he finished his im-promptu recital. Sniffling, Sunny couldn't help but ask what the difference between whiskey and bourbon and rye is. Ronny looked in the rearview like, "these guys serious?"

Ronny: "For a whiskey to call itself bourbon, the mash, the mixture of grains from which the product is distilled, must contain at least fifty-one percent corn. The rest of the mash is usually filled out with malted barley and either rye or wheat."

"So what's the deal with Scotch then?"

"The main difference between Scotch and whiskey is geographic, but also ingredients and spellings. Scotch is whisky without the e made in Scot-land. Bourbon is whiskey made in the states, generally in God's country."

"Kentucky," Sunny said.

Ronny: "Of course. Scotch is made mostly from malted barley, while bourbon is distilled from corn. If you're in England and ask for a whisky, you'll get Scotch. But in Ireland, you'll get Irish whiskey."

Sunny: "Okay, now can you please delineate the difference between Tennessee Whiskey, like Jack Daniel's and bourbon?

"Of course. After the spirit is distilled, Tennessee Whiskey is filtered through sugar-maple charcoal. This filtering is known as the Lincoln County Process. That's it for what distinguishes Tennessee Whiskey from your average bourbon, like Jim Beam. And if you're at all curious about the name, bourbon, it comes from an area known as Old Bourbon, around what is now Bourbon County, northwest of Lexington."

"Okay, what about Rye?" The Canadian asked.

"Rye whiskey must be distilled from at least 51 percent rye...see how this starts to work?"

By the time Ronny was done with his lecture, we'd arrived at Churchill Downs. Ronny stopped the car out front, where there was a stream of people in outrageous outfits meandering their way over to the main entrance. Lots of hoots and hollers.

"Fellas, it's been a pleasure."

"Here's to Old Kentucky," I said as I passed around Old Fitz for one more with our friend Ronny.

"Lads," he said from inside his car as we walked away. We turned to look. "Enjoy yourselves."

Hats. Big, boisterous, colourful hats. Wide-brimmed, narrow-brimmed, felt, straw, silk, some with long pieces of ribbon wildly tied together, some without. Women, young and old, they all wore them. Hats and dresses and high heels and accessories. Every single woman at the Kentucky Derby will have you thinking you left your heart in Louisville on your journey home. It was just past noon when we walked through the main gates. Already, three races had occurred. Already, the track was a pit of mud. The rains had only worsened. Sunny and I had to sneak Old Fitz and Billy Boy in with us. There is a strict rule forbidding any outside alcohol inside Churchill Downs. Ten races remained before the final race.

Sunny and I went straight to the nearest bar for our first mint juleps. I'd be lying if I said we weren't already well on our way to being juiced. The only thing we cared about was getting our bets in before the train was completely off the tracks. Mint juleps in hand, we trundled out to the rain-soaked in-field. It was bedlam in there. The degree of public intoxication was staggering. Mostly it was young, cheap people, like us. Lots of college kids, frat boys, sorority girls. The stands, we looked back at them with envy. There was a roof over those stands. Must be nice. We watched a couple races out there trying to not be distracted by the behaviour around us. Sunny and I both had an inkling that that too could be us after a couple more juleps. I requested Ol' Billy to charge up my first one. Sunny administered.

"You know I forgot to tell you something," he said as put away the glowing bottle.

"What's that?"

"When I woke up before you in the cave, that's when I first met Bill."

"What do you mean?"

"Well, he was walking out from the depths of the cave. And he walked straight by us without so much as a head nod. It was strange."

"You mean he was coming from deep within the cave?"

"I guess so. When I went to the campground, he was sitting there in his office, smilin' a big toothy grin toward me."

"Really?"

"Yeah."

"God, that's weird."

"Anyway, here's some more Ol' Billy for ya." I tipped a bit in my julep and then motioned the bottle toward Sunny. We were about halfway through the bottle now. We drank our juleps and there was no need to wince despite the astronomical alcohol content.

"You notice the colours are more vivid?"

"You noticed that too, huh?"

"Everyone looks...magnificent today..."

"I think we better go place our—" before I could finish my sentence, a lovely young woman appeared directly before us. She was tanned, blonde, wore red lipstick, was dressed in gold and white and her hat was the size of a sombrero.

"Ya'll's first time isn't it? I'm Scarlet. Like O'Hara, that's right. Welcome to Louisville. Isn't this rain a drag? Aren't these people animals? I just saw a kid I grew up with run across the roofs of that row of outhouses over there without any clothes on. Security didn't do a thang. Please, follow me." Before Sunny and I could think to say anything, she was dragging Sunny by the arm and I was following.

Scarlet said, "We'll talk when we're dry. Just follow me."

She walked us through Churchill Downs' innards. We had to fight our way through the masses. The relentless rains had most people inside. Eventually, Scarlet led us to a staircase guarded by security. She had to only bat those big eyelashes of hers a few times to get us through and up into the stands. It was that easy. Up we walked several floors and into the stands. Sunny and I were awestruck. Scarlet had led us to some of the best seats in the stands.

"Who are you?"

"Scarlet. And I do apologize, but I don't think we've met yet."

Sunny and I introduced ourselves. We told her pieces of how and why we got to Louisville. Scarlet just nodded politely as if to patiently wait until it was her turn to speak.

"Well, I'm from Louisville, and I know outta towners when I see 'em."

Sunny: "That obvious?"

"Looks like ya'll just went to a Dillard's or something. By the way, I would conceal that bottle of yours a little more, just sayin'…they don't like any other brands in here other than Woodford." I looked behind and she was right. Old Fitz was plainly evident in my back pocket.

"Well, how about we watch a race and then go place some bets?"

"Ya'll need help with those bets?"

"I think we're covered," Sunny said.

"Ya'll hear about the late entry? Never happens. I can't remember when the last time it happened. I been comin' to the Derby since I was a little girl."

"What late entry?"

"Some horse got in the final race, you know, the run for the roses, on a late entry…everyone's talkin' about it."

"Well Justify is still favoured to win isn't he?"

"Oh, of course. This new horse, the oddsmakers aren't giving the poor thing a hope in hell, pardon my language…got a weird name too…Shey Goompa or somethin'…daddy texted me said it was Buddhist or somethin' I don't know…let's go place some bets now that we have these seats."

Scarlet led us back into the building and we went to the nearest window. Sunny and I couldn't believe it. Shey Gompa! The same horse Schiffer, the jockey full of bourbon recommended.

I asked Scarlet, "You here with any friends, or you just like helpin' random strangers get outta the rain and into the stands?"

"Course I am. They're all around. My boyfriend and his friends are up in the Turf Club right now. We could get ya in if ya want."

"What's that?"

"Just a place where rich people like showing off is all. My boyfriend likes to think he's rich and a part of the club. His daddy is quite rich though, but that don't mean Ken's rich. Course I'm not complainin'. We're all going to Maui tomorrow for two weeks. You *must* meet Clara."

At the window, Sunny and I, not quite three sheets but certainly well past the point of no return, just wrote down a bunch of random bets on a bunch of different tickets. We placed Exactas, Win, Place, Shows, Superfectas, Across the Boards, all kinds of bets on each of the races leading up. Despite agreeing to focus our money on a few select bets, we didn't do that. It was a rodeo the way we bet our ten grand. So much for strategizing. Although, to shoot from the hip, there's a romance in that. Scarlet saw the money we were betting and she looked at us a different way from that point forward.

"Would you like to come to the Turf Club right now or spend some time in the stands," she said, doughy eyed. Sunny and I couldn't understand this lady. Why us? In any event, She got us to where we now were. Chalk it up to Southern hospitality.

The last bet I remember making was my last hundred bucks on a Superfecta. Shey Gompa number one, Justify at two, Good Magic at three, and Audible at four. Sunny and Scarlet both thought I was mad in making such a foolish bet. Just you wait and see, I said to them. Scarlet, I noticed, had her fingers in Sundance's belt loop. He didn't seem to mind.

We watched a couple of races from our seats. We never got a clear idea of who Scarlet was. All she said was that she worked in marketing. I told Sundance and Scarlet that I was going to the restroom and then find food. We hadn't eaten since the Super 8 continental breakfast. They were just fine sitting there, talking, getting close. I looked at the Kid and shook my inebriated head. He was just smiling away. The Kid was enjoying the attention. When I stood up to leave, whoever was standing behind me tapped my shoulder. I turned around to a big jovial man wearing a flat-brimmed straw hat.

"Hey mister," he said.

"Sorry, just on my way out."

"You tell me what the brand of whiskey is in the back of your pocket and I'll git you in the Turf Club with us."

"Pardon me?"

"Tell me the brand. If it's the right one, I'll get you to where there's a gourmet buffet, and bottomless juleps."

Scarlet turned to see what the commotion was about.

"Is there a problem here, sir? These are our seats, you know."

"Not askin' about the seats. Name's Heth. Henry Heth. How do ya do?" Heth took Scarlet's hand.

"Hello Mr. Heth. I'm Scarlet, this here's Mike and Sammy."

"He tells me the right brand of whiskey in his back pocket there..."

"I heard," Scarlet said.

"Old Fitz," I blurted out to the frustration of Scarlet.

"You say it's Old Fitzgerald?"

"Sure is. Here, take a swig, you want."

"No sir, that's not for me, and not the right answer." Heth laughed as his party got up to leave. "Here's my card for when you learn what the right whiskey is." Henry Heth turned out to be one of the top dogs at Woodford Reserve.

Scarlet said, "I knew it!"

"What do you mean you knew?"

"I snuck us into one of the most exclusive sections. Of course, people like Heth are gonna be sittin' here. What other brand of whiskey you think?"

Sunny said, "Guys, calm down! Please."

Scarlet: "And had you not blurted out what you said, I woulda gotten all of us in the Turf Club no problem at all. Now I think I can only get one of you in as my boyfriend."

"What will your actual boyfriend think?" Sunny asked.

"He don't care. He's too drunk to care by now anyway. That's really why I'm hangin' with ya'll. All my friends can barely stand at this point."

"Well," I said, "I'm starving. I'm gonna go and get some food and meet you two here later, okay?"

I never made it back to the seats. It took me almost an hour to wait in line for one measly hot dog. Sunny texted me while I was waiting to say he was in the Turf Club. Just finished a three-course seated lunch. Escargot, salmon, risotto, San Francisco sourdough. Was I angry? Sure. But then, had it been me, I'm sure I would've done the same. I was now my own. I went over to the Turf Club entrance to get an idea of how difficult it would be to sneak in. There were four guards standing shoulder to shoulder. The people they were letting through showed a different coloured lanyard than the ones given to us common folk. Hopeless.

Truth told, it's difficult to remember all that happened between the time Sunny and I finally met up again. I wandered a lot. Ate, drank and talked to a lot of strangers. Went out to the infield and watched those who didn't mind the downpour (it never let up the entire day). Sunny found me with an hour remaining before the big one. The run for the roses.

I was stumbling my way by the Turf Club entrance talking with a salty old New Yorker about horse doping. This was the kind of guy you see at the regional tracks, where there is absolutely no glamour. The kind of guy that really understands the odds and takes betting seriously. He had a moustache, Hawaiian shirt, slacks and a Panama hat. He'd been around the sport for five decades. He said one way trainers doped horses was with sodium bicarbonate nasal spray. Baking soda. The way it works, it neutralizes acid in muscle cells by raising the pH of the blood. This delays the onset of fatigue in a working muscle, permitting the horse to go longer at a peak rate of endurance.

"You think Zen Master was clean?"

"That's a can of worms. I do not know."

"How so?"

"They train their horses totally different than all the rest of the entire sport, you know."

"How so?"

"I really don't know. It's all just rumour. What I do know though, is trainers like Baffert haven't really changed their techniques since the '50s. There's been no science."

"You think they have a chance with their lawsuit?"

"Dunno, kid. Apparently, they have a horse in this race, but they kept it a secret which one. They wanna keep the PR down to a minimum. Anyway, my wife wants me back at the seats. Gotta go kid. Good luck."

It was dumb luck Sunny saw me talking, walking with the guy. Sunny called out and I turned to see him as he headed back to the Turf Club. His shirt was half untucked, unbuttoned to the breast bone. His cheeks were rosy.

"Meko! There you are you sonnavabitch! Been lookin' all over for you."

"Where've you been? I've just been wandering around last couple hours."

"You gotta come up to the Turf Club. I'm tellin' ya, it's just the best."

"Well, shit, I'll go right now, but I don't have a goddamn way in! You moron."

"Hang on. I'm sorry. I'll get Scarlet to get you in. Meko, you gotta get up here!"

Just like that, Sunny was gone again. Oblivious to the situation. I stood there for a few minutes and right as I was about to resume my wandering, I heard a voice call my name.

"There's my hubby!" Scarlet, of course. To my surprise, her togetherness remained intact. Unlike Sunny. With her on my arm, past the four big guards we marched up to the hallowed Turf Club. It was that easy.

"Sunny told me more about your trip," Scarlet said. "You actually played the blues in Edgewood? Burned the house down over a girl?" The Turf Club was a big room with huge windows overlooking the track below. Televisions were set up all over broadcasting the races. There were multiple bars and buffet tables. The people looked better, dressed better, drank more and ate more.

"Is that Paul Sorvino?" I said to Scarlet.

"Yes, he and his wife come every year. Over there is the Olympic skier, Bode, you may know of him? He's got a horse in the race."

"And where's Sunny? Your boyfriend?"

"I introduced him to a few of my girlfriends. They sure like Sunny. Sunny sure likes them. Ken is with his father in a different club. More exclusive than this one. Ugh."

"Let me get you a julep for getting me up here."

"Ha! It's free-pour up here, darlin'. You don't need to buy me anything. How ya'll been doing on your bets?"

"Haven't kept track. I've been watching the people more than the horses."

"Not uncommon. Let me take you to Sunny. He said he wants you to meet Clara. Said you'd like Clara."

"I'm gonna get drinks to bring over. See ya over there."

Scarlet was right. It was free-pour up in the Turf Club. As I waited for the bartender, the buffet caught my eye. Lobster, filet mignon, barbecue. Meeting Clara could wait. When I finally made it over to Sunny & Co., the most exciting two minutes in sports was moments from happening. The rains hadn't let up and here I was drying off, warming up in the Turf Club with an unlimited supply of fine food and booze.

Sunny was telling jokes, back slappin', being a real charmer to Scarlet's friends.

"Meko! You made it!"

"Here, I got ya'll another mint julep in case ya'll are thirsty." The bartender brought a tray of drinks to the table. Sunny gave me a hug and yelled, "This here's my cousin, who I think of as a brother! His name is Meko Torres!" And then to me: "Meko, I need to introduce you to someone."

"Clara?"

"How'd you know?"

"Wild guess."

"No shit, well anyway, you two are perfect for each other."

"No pact at the Derby?"

Sunny whispering, "Meko, it's Derby Day chrissake. I don't know. Ol Billy Boy, by the way, she gets the juices flowing, if ya know what I mean! Here have some. There's only a bit left."

Sunny either had almost half the bottle or shared it with others. I didn't care. I was three sheets by then anyway. Before I finished the last of it, I made a toast.

"Sunny, let's make a toast to this wild trip we've been on. Who knows about what tomorrow will bring, who knows what tonight will bring. Who in God's name knows what's gonna happen with this race that should happen any minute now. And most importantly, who knows if Von Rotz will be okay. But at least we are here now. And we've made our bets."

Scarlet said, "Who's Von Rotz?"

Sunny: "I like it. Okay, hang on, if I know you, I know what toast you're going to make."

Sunny and I said it together, the one our friend Von Rotz had taught us: "The standing toast that pleased the most was: the wind that blows, the ship that goes, and the lass that loved a sailor!" We clinked our silver cups after I poured what remained of Ol' Billy in them. Down the hatch. And then Sunny and I both dipped the girls to whom we delivered passionate kisses. After which, I introduced myself to Clara. We laughed. Not for long, however. The call to post interrupted. Up everyone now stood for the singing of *My Old Kentucky Home.* All 160,000 plus in attendance broke into song as the horses vying for the garland of roses walked their way onto the track.

"Sunny, look!"

"Is that?"

"Schiffer!" Our jockey full of bourbon was on the television. He was leading Shey Gompa out to the start gate and was having trouble walking a straight line.

The sun shines bright in the old Kentucky home,
Tis summer, the people are gay;
The corn-top's ripe and the meadow's in the bloom
While the birds make music all the day.
The young folks roll on the little cabin floor
All merry, all happy and bright;
By'n by hard times comes a knocking at the door
Then my old Kentucky home, Good-night!
Weep no more my lady.
Oh! Weep no more today!
We will sing one song for the old Kentucky home
For the old Kentucky home, far away.

...And they're off!

FEBRUARY 1

Dear Lula Mae,

Understandably, you were miffed that I wasn't able to finish the story in that last letter. That was how he left it with me too. He said he'd leave the rest for when we made our return to Taos from Aspen. Well, here I am in Taos writing you this final letter about Meko and Sunny's Run For Roses. The final leg went well down from Colorado to Taos. Spectacular scenery as you drive alongside the Sangre de Cristos. You need to do this road trip sometime. We are in Taos now - arrived last night. Meko is itching to get back on the road already. I can't report much about this place other than, yes it's enchanted, yes there is adobe architecture everywhere, and yes there's just as many art galleries. It's a town unlike any I've ever seen before. So different from the Pacific Northwest.

Oh, and apparently he accepted the job to go to Aspen in October. So now he's figuring out his exit strategy with his girlfriend? I think, anyway. I don't know. I don't know if he knows. Yes, they are back together and no, she doesn't yet know about Aspen. I know, it's crazy. But Meko, as we both know, he shoots from the hip. I think I'm returning north once spring hits and the heat starts...heating up. The weather is great right now. I think Meko will take me up past Arroyo Seco to the ski hill for a tour later this week. Till next time...

Yours,
Foxworth

* * *

How the cousins ended up in the Bronx at a Yankees game before Meko partially resolved a key unanswered question on Bleeker Street in the Village.

The stadium lights shined bright. From where we sat, we could make out the player's last names. For the Red Sox, that is. Yankees home jerseys have only numbers on the back. Sunny had arrived to Yankees Stadium before me. In the time it took for me to arrive, he scalped us our tickets. I think it was like eighty bucks each. We didn't think we'd get any. After all, it was the Yankees playing the Red Sox!

Before entering the stadium, we ate Big Macs on a picnic table among kids from the Bronx. There we were in the gritty Bronx. Going to watch a ball game. Between bites, we caught up a bit but not much. I think we both wanted to save it for the game. I asked him what of Manhattan he'd seen. He looked at me like, burger first, talk later. Fine. For him, it was his first time in New York. It was my second. But it still felt like my first. The scale of Manhattan to a kid from Arroyo Seco is breathtaking.

Sunny and I arrived to New York on different flights on different days. Just the way the flights worked out given our final destinations. His route home to Calgary International had him laid over in Manhattan for a couple days before a stopover in Chicago and then north across the border to Alberta. From LaGuardia, I had a flight to Denver the next day and from Denver, a flight down to Taos.

"Not bad seats."

"Yeah. You nervous at all when they scanned those tickets? I was."

"Never know with scalped, you're right."

"You ever been to a ball game?"

"Never. You?"

"Went to a Giants game once in SF. Tickets were two bucks. No joke."

"How does this sport stay alive?"

Watching a baseball game is conducive to conversation. There's plenty of time between the action. Being an early season game, the stakes were low. Hell, those guys have close to two hundred games to get through before the end of the year, not counting playoffs. We got to our seats before the national anthem. With all of the formalities out of the way, we were left to sit and watch a baseball game. Sit there and listen to New Yorkers yell obscenities toward Dustin Pedroia. And cheer when Stanton smashed a homer in the fourth. That guy is paid handsomely. Good work if you can get it. Before Stanton hit his homer, Sunny said he was thinking of adopting a couple dogs when he got home. I was surprised, but encouraging. I guess his girlfriend had sent him a photo of a couple dogs new to the local SPCA. They were rescue dogs from a Milk River puppy mill. I told him they'd have a good life on his ranch. He asked if I ever wanted a dog. Of course, I told him.

"LEMONADE, LEMONADE! JUST LIKE GRAMMA MADE!"

Sunny said, "You want a lemonade?"

"Nah, let him pass. I'll get us a couple beers when they come around."

"Let me get it. I still got some winnings from the Derby."

"Yeah?"

"How about you?"

"Broke even...I think."

"Can't believe they DQ'd him."

"Yeah. No way did he cross the line."

Shey Gompa, to the surprise of all 160,000 in attendance at Churchill Downs, and all the millions who watched on TV, made all the other horses, Justify included, look amateur. That's how dominant he was. That three year old horse commanded the Derby's two million dollar purse. The twenty-five thousand dollar entrance fee? Chump change. He crossed the finish line six and a quarter lengths ahead of the rest. But, early in the race, before the first turn, video evidence showed that he may have crossed the line and impeded Promises Fulfilled, a long shot who finished way out. I say may because the footage was so poor, so rain socked, so muddied, it was far from incriminating.

It took about eighteen hours for the powers that be to officially disqualify Shey Gompa. Down the drain went the eye-popping figure I'd won. The odds on my Shey Gompa bet were so low that the winnings were astronomical. I was the only one to make the bet. I do not wish to share the amount that was taken away from me. It's too painful. Let me just say that it would have taken care of any experimental treatment of Von Rotz's choosing and *Alysheba*. Of course, Sunny and I found out that Justify won the race the next day while in Lexington. We had a day to kill before I flew the next day to Manhattan. Sunny flew to New York the day after.

Nursing considerable hangovers after a wild Saturday night on Bardstown Road, we sought refuge in the Kentucky countryside. We invited the girls, they being Scarlet and Clara to come along, but they were all off to Maui first thing Sunday morning. Clara said she'd text me when they arrived. I never again heard from her. Oh well, fun while it lasted dirty dancing our night away in O'Shea's Pub. That bar, *the* bar, didn't close that night. We were in Europe. All night and into the wee hours, it was one helluva of a party. Music, food, dancing. And the rains never stopped.

Sunday morning, it was bright blue and sunny. Naturally. Despite all the gravity in the world keeping us bedridden in our mess of a Super 8 hotel room, Sunny and I managed to saddle up and head east toward Lexington. Rolling, green hills. Horse farm after horse farm. We drove by gated Win Star Farms. Justify's home base. We bore witness to true bluegrass country. The Promised Land. Versailles and Frankfort, distillery after distillery. We toured Bulleit, Four Roses, Wild Turkey. We drank more bourbon. On an old brick wall of one of the distillers, I can't remember which, was the following:

We make fine bourbon
At a profit if we can
At a loss if we must
But always
Fine Bourbon

I have a love affair with the land around Lexington. We went to check out the classy Keeneland track, just outside Lexington. If Churchill Downs is going to MSG to see the Stones, Keeneland is going to Radio City Music Hall to see Derek Trucks. At that point, we still were waiting on the decision, like the rest of the horse racing world. I walked into the empty Keeneland track and stood in the middle. I imagined myself riding a horse like Shey Gompa with the crowds roaring, the light bulbs flashing, the garland of roses in my arms. As Sunny and I rambled our way back toward Louisville, the news came in over the radio. Sunny had to pull over on the side of the road. It was a tough moment.

The Yankees beat the Red Sox that night. They were down most of the game but made their comeback in the eighth inning. The Cuban flamethrower, Aroldis Chapman, closed the win out for the pinstripes. He was somehow throwing 110 mile an hour fastballs that night. What hope did the Sox have? As we watched the game, we talked about Manhattan. We both rode Citibikes up and down Fifth Avenue and all over. We wondered how we didn't cross paths. Museum of Natural history, MOMA, SoHo, the canyons of lower Manhattan, Midtown, Central Park, between the two of us, we saw a lot. There's something special about that city that never sleeps. And as we exited the ballpark toward the subway, we had a few good laughs.

"Remember when we were on Frenchman? Or how about Chauncey!"

Sunny: "Remember that meal we had in Demopolis? The full moon as we drove to Tuscaloosa and can you believe you played on stage in Atlanta?"

196 · James Rose

"Gina!"

"How about the Waffle House!"

Together: "Shaunice!"

Sunny said he spoke with his mom earlier that day. She told him that Von Rotz's condition was no better. But she said that when she went to tell him of our trip to the Derby, whereas before he was pretty well lifeless. After she told our story, with eyes closed, he managed a smile. Not a big one, but smile nonetheless. Sunny told me that as we waited for the subway back to Manhattan. It was emotional.

Sunny said, "We tried."

"And we had fun."

"Meko, if there's anything I've learned, it's the journey, man. We gotta enjoy this journey."

We didn't say much more until Sunny got off at his stop. We were made silent by our thoughts on the southbound train. He'd found a cheap Airbnb in Harlem. I was staying with a friend way down in the Lower East Side. When the time came, Sunny struggled through the crowded train toward the open door. He stepped out, turned around, stood on the platform and looked in as the doors closed.

At Grand Central, I switched trains. I almost went down the wrong staircase among the flurry of people scrambling toward different platforms. The green line was far less busy. I found a seat and grew restless. I stood to look at an overhead map - only a few more stops. I sat back down.

In twenty-four hours, I'd be back in Taos. Back to the same old. Before I let myself start to dwell, I saw him. He was sitting directly across from me, reading the New York Times. Decker. I couldn't see his face, but I recognized the black fedora, grey trench coat. He must've felt my eyes on him as he lowered the paper to look at me with cold precision.

"Long way from Nashville," I said. He grinned. The train stopped and he stood up to go.

"Let's go for a walk," he said.

"This Bleeker? I'm not for another few."

"Let's go for a walk."

Decker and I walked west from the metro station. A slow, contemplative walk. "You're wondering what more I have to say to you."

"Wondering a lot of things."

"Ask me anything."

"Shey Gompa was obviously your horse, did he DQ?"

"Hard to tell. That's horse racing."

"That jockey full of bourbon, Schiffer, he sure didn't help. I saw him stagger onto the track."

"Aw Schiffer was fine. True he likes his bourbon. But I won't getting in his way about that. He's his own man, one of the best you know."

"You don't seem to care."

"Care about what?"

"About winning?"

"Oh, we won. Everyone knows that."

"What do you mean?"

"Did you watch the race?"

"Of course."

"You saw how much further ahead our horse was, didn't you? Let me ask you something."

"Okay..."

"Your friend Von Rotz, he gonna be okay?"

"Doesn't sound like it."

"Damn. Thought he'd come through. That's life, I guess." Decker smiled.

"You're not at all mad at Justify winning?"

"No. You know he failed a drug test, didn't you?"

"What?"

"Few weeks ago at the Santa Anita Derby. There's been a cover-up. He shouldn't have been allowed to enter the race on Saturday. Scopolamine was what they gave him, and they'll just say it was from the jimson weed he'd been eating. It's to clear a horse's airway, optimize the animal's heart rate. More efficient."

"This is Rowan Oak territory."

"The investors behind him, the TV networks, there's more to horse racing than bread and water. You know anyone at the Times? You're a journalist, right?" Decker was nearly laughing as he told me this. Didn't seem to care. Zen.

"Back up. You can't just dangle that in front of me."

"It'll come out eventually. I just thought you may be interested in the story."

"That can't be what you meant this whole time? About helping you and your business partner?"

"No. I think you should write our story. I figured if you won money, you'd want to write about it. I know you to be honest. I think you'd tell our story well and I know the power of the written word in the court of public opinion. "

"Why me?"

"I was skiing up in Montana this winter. In one of those state-wide life-style magazines, I read your story about wild horses. Thought it was great, looked you up after."

"I'm flattered."

"You're a skier. You know Bode, right?"

"Know of him, yes."

"You ever wonder where he gets his horse racing ideas from?"

"About?"

"You don't know?"

"No, I don't know anything about horse racing."

"Progress and improvement takes time in horse racing. It's a sport that can be deceiving. You and I can buy into a horse today for five grand. That horse will be within 5% of Justify or American Pharaoh or any of the best of the best. Justify can run a mile and a sixteenth in one minute forty. A horse of mine purchased for fifteen grand can run the same distance in one minute, forty-three. That's a 3% difference. And that's with a status quo training program that hasn't changed in sixty years. No modern sport science used. We've proven that there is no way thoroughbred horses today are at the peak of their physical condition. Consider that the 1950 Derby winner was two seconds faster than the 2017 winner. The margin of victory is very slim.

At Tassajara, we're certainly not made of money. Far wealthier barn owners are already established and have their top trainers, the Bob Baffert's of the world. All things equal, buying a better horse works. If everyone's doing the same thing training, then the better horses win and they can be purchased by those with the money. In 2017, one of Bode's horses, En Hanse, earned his first career victory in his fourth start when he led from start to finish to win a sprint at a race at Churchill Downs. He followed with a runaway win before an unplaced finish in his stakes debut. Bode got his training ideas from us and from his career in skiing. We've been pioneering a modern sport science approach to training horses for thirty years. Only in the last few years have we been showing our horses at the big events.

But there's certainly no guarantee that if you were to pay a three-hundred thousand stud fee for a horse from one of the country's top studs, you'll end up with a winning horse. Statistically, it's a very difficult sport. Of the 40,000 or so that are born each year, less than a thousand win a race of any sort. And 1% of that win a stakes race. No one really knows how good a horse is until they're in a race. Because they're all so close. The best horses in the world often have the exact same times as lesser horses in training.

Anyway, that's enough for now. Come visit out at my place in Carmel. Take care, Meko." Decker waved a cab down and was about to climb in before I asked one more question. "What's with the Buddhist theme?"

He laughed. "Dunno, just thought it sounded cool. My wife and bought an old Buddhist retreat called Tassajara few years back. East of Carmel. It's where our barn is now. Come visit sometime. Tell our story. Sell it to some fancy New York publisher for some coin. You still got my card?" Decker sped off.

It was past midnight. I couldn't quite wrap my head around what I'd just heard. I started to laugh. And then I heard something I hadn't heard in a while. I heard singing.

You made me cry
When you said goodbye
Ain't that a shame?

I turned around. Decker left me standing in front of a club called Domino's. There was live music inside. The kind you hear down in New Orleans. Tubas, trumpets, clarinets, a shuffled beat. On the street by the club's entrance, a sandwich board advertised the evening drink special. Sazerac Night. I walked in.

ACKNOWLEDGEMENTS

Thank you Mom for proofreading and feedback.

Thank you Sarah Bennett for another great cover design.

Thank you Jesse Gordon for another superb job formatting this book.

Thank you Trevor for joining me on the trip that inspired this crazy story.

ABOUT JAMES

James grew up in British Columbia's Columbia Valley and holds a bachelor's degree in commerce from the University of Calgary. As a journalist, James has written for the *Financial Post*, *Aspen Daily News*, *Calgary Herald*, *Forecast Ski Magazine*, *Columbia Valley Pioneer*, and *BOEReport.com*. In 2018, James completed a residency in Environmental Reportage at the *Banff Centre for Literary Arts*. As an alpine ski racing coach, James has worked with *Team Panorama Ski Club* and *Aspen Valley Ski and Snowboard Club*. James co-founded *rose bros coffee* with his brother, Trevor. In January, 2021, James enrolled at the Vancouver Film School to study writing for film and television. *Run For Roses* is James' third book.

jamesrosewrites.com
ig/fb/tw: jamesrosewrites

www.ingramcontent.com/pod-product-compliance
Lightning Source LLC
Chambersburg PA
CBHW032117020726
47494CB00007BA/2115